Dear Little Black Dre~~ss~~

Thanks for picking u~~p~~ ~~one~~ of the great new titles ~~in our series of~~ fun, page-turning romance novels. Lucky you — you're about to have a fantastic romantic read that we know you won't be able to put down!

Why don't you make your Little Black Dress experience even better by logging on to

www.littleblackdressbooks.com

where you can:

- Enter our **monthly competitions** to win **gorgeous** prizes
- Get **hot-off-the-press** news about our latest titles
- Read **exclusive** preview chapters both from your **favourite** authors and from brilliant new writing talent
- Buy **up-and-coming** books online
- Sign up for an essential slice of romance via our **fortnightly email** newsletter

We love nothing more than to curl up and indulge in an addictive romance, and so we're delighted to welcome you into the Little Black Dress club!

With love from,

The *little black dress* team

Five interesting things about Janet Mullany:

1. My favourite books are *Wives and Daughters* by Mrs Gaskell, because it is so lush and romantic; *Vilette* by Charlotte Brontë for its passion and subversiveness; and *Emma* by Jane Austen, for its perfect plotting.

2. On the other hand, my commuter reading tends to be the same sort of stuff everyone reads, and my rating system for good reads includes missed stops (very good) and wrong lines (very, very good).

3. Once, staying overnight in an old house, I woke up and heard someone breathing. I was alone in the room. I got out fast.

4. I like tea. I mean, really like tea. I get mean if I don't get enough.

5. When I was five my brother pushed me into a tadpole pond. To this day he denies it.

Fine out more about Janet at www.janetmullany.com
and riskyregencies.blogspot.com

By Janet Mullany

The Rules of Gentility
A Most Lamentable Comedy
Improper Relations
Mr Bishop and the Actress

Mr Bishop
and the Actress

Janet Mullany

little
black
dress

First published in Great Britain in 2011 by
LITTLE BLACK DRESS
An imprint of HEADLINE PUBLISHING GROUP

A LITTLE BLACK DRESS paperback

1

Cataloguing in Publication Data is available from the British Library

ISBN 978 0 7553 4781 0

Typeset in Transit511BT by Avon DataSet Ltd,
Bidford-on-Avon, Warwickshire

Printed and bound in Great Britain by
Clays Ltd, St Ives plc

HEADLINE PUBLISHING GROUP
An Hachette UK Company
338 Euston Road
London NW1 3BH

www.littleblackdressbooks.com
www.headline.co.uk
www.hachette.co.uk

To the Tarts

Acknowledgements

Thanks to Lucienne and the Little Black Dress team; the staff at the Regency Town House, Brighton; Pam, Miranda, and all my other writing buddies; Alison, Steve, and all the usual suspects.

Prologue

Miss Lewisham's Academy for Gentlewomen, 1799

Sophie clung to the ladder, her face a pale oval in the dark as she looked up at the two girls peering out of the window. 'Promise me we shall always be friends.'

'Yes, yes. But hurry!'

Captain Wallace's cigar streaked through the air like a small comet as he tossed it aside and crushed it beneath a well-polished regimental boot. 'Come along, Sophie my love, there's a good girl.'

'Sssh!' Claire and Lizzie said together.

They could hear sounds of activity from downstairs, the rattle of a poker in a grate and the scrape of a chair on a wooden floor.

Claire pushed Lizzie aside, Sophie's trunk in her arms. 'Catch, Captain!'

Sophie gave a small shriek as her possessions hit her beloved in the midriff. He sat down heavily, saying some words unfamiliar to the three young ladies.

Sophie took a step up the ladder, one slender hand reached out.

'What are you *doing*?' Claire tried to push her back down. 'You promised him! You can't—'

'My bonnet. You have forgotten my new bonnet.'

Claire looked around the room, snatched up a hat box, and hurled it out of the window.

Below, a spill of warm golden light on to the ground indicated that someone, probably Miss Lewisham herself, had lit a lamp to investigate the strange noises outside, which now included the audible swearing of the muddy and lovestruck Captain.

'Always! Promise me!' Sophie said.

'Yes, we shall always be friends. But please hurry, Sophie.'

She took a step down the ladder. 'In five years?'

'Yes.'

'Ten? Fifteen?'

'Damnation,' said Claire, a daring word used for special occasions only, then whispered out of the window, 'Lewisham is coming upstairs. We'll always love you, Sophie, we'll always be best friends. Please go.' She hissed to Lizzie, 'Lady Macbeth!'

The stair creaked as Miss Lewisham ascended.

'I beg your pardon?'

'As we arranged! Lady Macbeth! Sleepwalk, Lizzie.'

'I can't! Why don't *you* sleepwalk?'

'We agreed, in dire emergency, if Lewisham awoke—'

'No!'

'Running outside the room and vomiting, then.'

'Absolutely not.'

'You promised', Claire whispered, 'that you would create a diversion if necessary. You were supposed to ask Skinny Letitia how to vomit at will. You—'

From outside Sophie squealed and Lizzie and Claire rushed to the window to see the Captain toss her into his curricle, where she landed sprawled in a disorder of petticoats, clutching at her hat. He leaped aboard and whipped his team into a gallop.

Lizzie took advantage of the commotion to pull the window shut and the curtains drawn. Outside Sophie's hatbox lay deserted in a puddle, forgotten as Captain Wallace and his intended bride rushed off to Gretna Green.

A door opened and closed as Miss Lewisham checked rooms.

Claire and Lizzie jumped into bed and composed themselves into the semblance of maidenly slumber. An effigy lay in Sophie's bed: a nightcap on the pillow, rolled-up cloaks beneath the sheets.

Their door creaked open to reveal Miss Lewisham in her night-time glory, her hair tied in multicoloured rags to achieve the rigid curl of daytime. The two girls slowed their breathing until the light of Miss Lewisham's candle faded as she closed the door behind her and continued down the corridor to find which of her chicks had flown the nest.

'Fifteen years,' Claire whispered. 'We'll be old. Thirty!'

They both giggled in horror.

'But we'll still all be friends,' Lizzie said.

'Still friends.' Claire yawned. 'So long as Sophie keeps her promise to tell us about the wedding night.'

They lay awake for a little, knowing they would be sent home in disgrace when Sophie's elopement and their roles as conspirators were revealed.

They entered the marriage mart armed with modest dowries, some prettiness, impeccable pedigrees, and the fragments of an imperfect education.

Claire made a brilliant match and Lizzie a respectable but modest one.

And Sophie . . . Sophie chose a different direction.

1814, Norfolk

Mr Harry Bishop

Viscount Shadderly's household, in which I have accepted the position of steward, is in a shocking state.

Three retired seamen who barely make a whole man between them, for one misses an eye, another a leg and the third an arm, are the footmen. I dread to think what will happen if they must carry soup. The upper footman, currently the most senior of the staff, is one Jeremiah whose lamentations about my departed predecessor centre chiefly on the gentleman's abnormally large feet, for Jeremiah considered himself the natural heir to Mr Roberts' cast-off boots. He regards my feet with dismay.

'It would never have done, sir, never, but I wish you the best of luck, sir.'

And so this is his last day in the house, for he and his new bride, formerly lady's maid to Lady Shadderly, are on their way to join Roberts and his supply of footwear in another household.

I agree with him that it certainly will not do, but for other reasons. Two small children in dresses sit on the kitchen table feeding raw pastry into their mouths; the elder, a child of four or so, is the heir to the Viscount Shadderly, or Lord Shad as he is referred to with great affection by the household staff. Since I have met his lordship only in an exchange of letters my impression is that his staff like him for the liberties he tolerates downstairs.

I am not sure of the gender of the other child, a couple of years younger, who begins a slow, perilous descent down the table leg, a large wooden spoon clutched in one hand. I move forward to rescue the infant, who rewards me with a piercing shriek and a blow to the nose with the spoon.

'Bless his heart!' Mrs Dawson the cook exclaims, answering my unspoken question, and scoops the child into her arms. 'Never you mind young Master Simon, Mr Bishop, he's the sweetest of children.'

Eyes watering, I nod in agreement. 'Where is their nursemaid?'

'Nursemaid? Oh, Lady Shad don't believe in them. We're always willing to help out with the little dears.

Now, Master George, you are not to pull the cat's tail so, you know she will scratch. They are to hire a governess for Miss Amelia, though, now she's almost a young lady.'

I pluck the cat from the table – a trail of footprints now adorn the pastry – and, as an afterthought, young Master George. He stares at me.

'I want Mama,' he announces as I plant him on the floor.

'Lord Shad's home,' the one-armed footman announces, placing his mug of ale on the kitchen table and attaching a hook before hastening upstairs to open the front door. Master George reaches for the ale and spills it down himself.

The kitchen lurches into action; the pastry is wiped off and placed into a pie dish, the boy at the spit wakes up and turns the meat, and one of the female staff takes the two dirty children upstairs to be presented to their parents. 'And Miss Amelia is . . . ?'

'Lord Shad's ward,' Mrs Dawson replies with a firmness that does not invite further questions. 'A very clever young lady, almost seventeen.' She turns away and bellows at the kitchen staff to fetch coals and cabbage. I make note of the cracked china, the tarnished silver, and the general dirt and disorder.

'Does the family always dine this early?' It's scarcely three o'clock.

'They keep country hours usually, but a troupe of

dancing dogs and a talking horse perform on the village green this evening and Lord Shad has given us permission to attend.'

'Indeed.' I should not have let this slovenly household have a night off, and I do not care that it shows on my face.

The footman returns with an order for tea upstairs and an invitation for me to dine with milord and milady. I'm somewhat taken aback at this egalitarianism, but this is the country after all.

I shall advise my employer and his lady to avoid the pie.

'Pie, Bishop?' Lady Shad waves a tarnished silver spoonful in my direction.

'Thank you, ma'am, I—'

She drops the spoonful on to my plate. 'Mrs Dawson has the lightest hand with pastry I have ever encountered.'

And possibly the dirtiest, although cooking has transformed that grey slab of dough into a wondrous golden flaky crust.

'Don't force food upon the man, Char. So as I was saying, Bishop, things have pretty much gone to seed since Roberts left.' Viscount Shadderly is a handsome man in his mid-thirties, some ten years older than me; his wife, an attractive, plain-spoken woman, is vastly pregnant. 'Meanwhile I regret I must leave for London tomorrow.'

'You must?' Lady Shad lurches to her feet, one hand on the table.

We both rise and watch her with some trepidation. Although she looks as though she is about to give birth at any moment, she has risen to spear another slice of ham from a platter.

'Yes, my love. This matter with Charlie. My nephew experiences some financial difficulties,' he explains to me as we sit.

'He's not your nephew. I believe he's some sort of third cousin,' Lady Shad comments. 'And he's become entangled with some elderly lightskirt who's put him deeply in debt and he's only twenty. But I don't think you'll go.'

'Why's that?' He looks at her, eyes narrowed.

She lays her hand upon her swollen belly. 'Oh, no particular reason. Pass the claret, if you will, Bishop.'

'What!' Lord Shad leaps to his feet, knocking a plate on to the floor. 'Are you in labour, ma'am?'

She shrugs. 'Don't concern yourself.'

'How long?'

'Oh, since about eleven this morning.'

'Ma'am, we have spent most of that time bumping along our abysmal country roads in a trap. Are you mad?'

'I thought it might help things along. Besides, I wanted to see Hopkins's new mare.'

Lord Shad mutters something about Hopkins's new mare be damned under his breath and I consider how best to extricate myself from this delicate situation. He turns to me and barks, 'Fetch Mrs Simpkins directly!'

'I beg your pardon, sir. Who is—'

Lady Shadderly pours herself a glass of claret. 'Of course he doesn't know who Mrs Simpkins is, Shad. She's the midwife.'

'And every time, ma'am, I've told you we should be in town for your lyings-in with an accoucheur, not that toothless gossip—'

Lady Shad stands and I wonder if she is about to throw something at her husband, but naturally we stand too. The lady lays a hand on her swollen abdomen and makes a sound I can only describe as a grunt. Her husband and I stand transfixed until she lets out her breath in a long sigh. 'That was a good one . . . Last time I saw her, Mrs Simpkins had six teeth.'

'Her teeth, ma'am, are immaterial. What is at stake now is whether Bishop can reach her in time. Well, man, off with you.'

'I beg your pardon, my lord.' I move towards the door. 'Where exactly will I find Mrs Simpkins?'

'Damnation. You take the road into the village but before you get there, when you come to the crossroads, there is a large elm tree on your right and—'

'Send a footman,' Lady Shad says.

'Excellent idea,' says Lord Shad.

'I beg your pardon, my lord, they're all at the village for the fair.'

'Who the devil gave them permission?' Lord Shad shouts.

'You did,' says Lady Shad. She rests her elbows on the back of her chair. 'Bishop, when you get there, make sure you see the mermaid.'

'What mermaid?' her husband asks.

'There's a mermaid . . .' A long pause as she bends her forehead to her fists. 'And dancing dogs and a talking horse.'

'For God's sake!' Lord Shad drains his glass of claret and bangs it on to the table. 'Bishop, be on your way.'

'Yes, my lord.'

'Don't be a fool,' Lady Shad says. 'He'll get lost. You go, Shad.'

Lord Shad looks from me to his wife and back again. He shakes his head. 'I see I have no choice. Very well. Bishop, do whatever she says. My dear, pray try not to have the child for an hour.'

They kiss each other with a tenderness that makes me uncomfortable, for clearly they are much in love and I feel like an interloper.

'Go away, Shad.' His lady pushes him from her. 'And don't forget the mermaid.'

He runs from the room, leaving me frozen in terror

while Lady Shad bends her head to the back of the chair again. I believe we are the only people in the house other than the children asleep upstairs. This was certainly not how I expected to begin my duties in the household. I had envisioned a quiet evening in the steward's house (now mine) and to bed early to make up for the last two nights: sleepless nights in which I travelled from the north of England to take this position.

'May I be of some assistance, ma'am?' I ask when she straightens up again.

'Give me your arm. I want to walk.' This is so unlike my very limited knowledge of childbirth – overheard, whispered fragmentary accounts of hours and days of screaming and clutching bedposts – that I am relieved, fool that I am. She leans on my arm and we pace up and down the room, pausing when her fingers grip my arm and she leans on me, breathing heavily. Now and again she curses.

'Do you think the mermaid is a girl with a fish tail?' she asks.

'Or the other way round, ma'am.'

She laughs a little and then groans and clutches my arm. 'Bishop, is the bowl the cabbage was served in empty?'

'You'd like some more cabbage, ma'am?'

'No. Hand me the damned bowl.'

She pushes past me to grab the bowl from the table and vomits copiously into it, to my horror. She appears most unwell, flushed and sweaty, but she looks at me with a weak smile. 'Don't be so alarmed, Bishop. We will not have much longer at this. I always puke at around this time.'

'That hardly reassures me, ma'am.' I take the bowl from her and hand her a napkin. 'What should I do?'

She shakes her head and takes my arm again. We resume our perambulation of the room while I hope desperately that her husband will return soon with the midwife who will take over from my male incompetence.

How long did he say he would be? An hour? There is no clock in the dining room. We walk and stop at her pains, and it seems to me that there is less walking now and more stopping.

'Ma'am, should you not retire to your bed?' Isn't that how women are supposed to do it?

'No. Don't want to mess up the bed hangings.' She stops at a sofa. 'I must sit.' I try to help her but she seems to have turned into a madwoman, pushing me away and cursing at me, and I fear the pangs of childbirth and the attentions of a stranger may have addled her mind.

'Don't touch me!' she shrieks. Then, quite rationally, 'Have you ever attended a birth before?'

'Only kittens.' And that was a much neater and tidier business, with the mother cat purring and producing a tidy bundle of kitten every minute or so.

'It hurts! Where's Shad?' She writhes and slips off the

edge of the sofa on to the floor, landing on her knees. At a loss, I moisten a napkin from the table with water and wipe her forehead, and as she does not scream at me I assume this helps.

'My skirts.' She rocks from side to side, attempting to free her skirts from under her knees. There is nothing for it now; apparently I am to become a man midwife whether I wish to or not, despite my terror.

'Pray don't distress yourself, ma'am.'

'You whoreson!' she screams at me, or her absent husband, or no one in particular. 'Get my skirts up, you fool. You know how to do that, don't you? This is no time for modesty.'

I can see that. 'To be perfectly honest, ma'am—'

'Hold your tongue!' Then, very loudly and with a deafening shriek, 'Do something!'

I tear off my coat for better access to her ladyship's nether regions.

'I shall die!' she screams.

And then her husband will kill me for sure, which he may do anyway.

She grabs my ear with one hand, the sofa with the other – the ancient brocade gives way under her nails – and dear God, someone else has joined us in a great rush of warm fluid. That is, I believe it to be a person, smeared in blood and some sort of wax, creased and hideous, slippery in my hands.

She stops screaming and the room is tremendously quiet. 'What is it?'

How can I tell her she has given birth to a monster? A twisted blue rope obscures its sex. 'I don't know. A boy? No, it's a girl. Yes, a girl.'

'Give her to me!' she screams very loudly, but it's a different, exultant sort of cry. The strange creature in my arms now flails its limbs and turns from grey to mottled red as it opens its mouth to shriek almost as loudly as its mother. From one second to another, everything is transformed.

'You're crying, Bishop,' Lady Shad says and reaches for the child we have just delivered.

I am, to my surprise. I also seem to have forgotten how to breathe and I can't see properly. Mother and child, the dining room with its cobwebbed comices and dark paintings on the wall, all spin around and away from me as I fall into an unmanly swoon.

'Bishop?' Lord Shad kneels at my side. He's smiling although somewhat wet around the eyes, and holds a glass of brandy. 'My apologies for leaving you in such a damnable situation, sir, and my most heartfelt thanks for the safe delivery of my daughter. Lady Shad has sung your praises this past quarter hour. We thought it best to let you sleep for a while.'

'The baby,' I croak. 'Lady Shad. Are they well? I beg

your pardon for falling asleep. I am somewhat fatigued.'

'They are both well, thanks to you. Come and drink my daughter's health.' He pats my shoulder and retreats.

The room is transformed. Before, I saw a slightly shabby dining room with dingy faded walls and indifferent portraits, dark with age, hung around it. Now it glows golden in lamplight, and Lady Shad sits on the couch, her daughter at her breast, her two little boys awed and adoring at her side, as beautiful as any portrait painting. A woman, who from her lack of teeth must be Mrs Simpkins, clucks over them all and urges Lady Shad to drink ale.

'My deliverer!' Lady Shad holds her hand out to me and laughs at her own joke. 'I must not laugh. It hurts my— well, never mind where it hurts, Bishop. Look at this child you and I produced.'

'I beg your pardon, ma'am. I believe I had some previous involvement in the matter,' Shad says. 'What shall we name her? What is your Christian name, Bishop?'

'Henry, my lord. My family call me Harry, but I beg of you, do not feel obliged—'

'Harry! Then she must be Harriet,' Lady Shad says. 'And we owe you a coat, Bishop. I'm afraid yours is ruined.'

The child, although still somewhat creased and red, has been wiped clean and looks slightly less like a goblin. I feel a great surge of pride and affection as though she were my own, and for Lady Shad too, whom I believe I must be halfway in love with, despite the indignities of our association. And I am more than halfway in love with the whole family, if such a thing is possible. I see now why Shad (and referring to him thus seems natural and easy) is so highly regarded downstairs, this man who has treated me with such kindness, and now sits with his two sons upon his lap gazing upon his wife and new daughter.

Shad raises his glass to me. 'Your health, Bishop. I regret I must send you to London to deal with my family matters, but there's no need to rush off soon. If Charlie's ruined, another week won't make much difference, and you should be here for your namesake's christening.'

Our raised glasses clink together. I am determined to do my utmost for the family that now feels like my own.

Mrs Sophie Wallace

'Sorry, darling, it's either you or the horses.'

We both flatten ourselves against the stairwell as two sweating bailiffs angle the sideboard, a hefty piece of furniture that Charlie chose but apparently never paid for, a florid masterpiece of inlay and gilding and bowed legs.

'At least, that's what my uncle's fellow downstairs says,' he adds, giving me the sort of smile that still makes me fizz a bit inside, charming, slightly lopsided, rueful, as he runs his hand through his blond hair. I remind myself that Charlie Fordham, my soon-to-be-ex-protector, is only twenty, almost a decade younger than me. This is his first year in London, and he has proved a delightful companion. I'm pretty sure his family will insist on finding him an heiress to marry, now Charlie has got into trouble and disgracefully into debt.

But he won't be married to me. I am not the sort of woman men like Charlie marry.

He's gazing at the sideboard, which is now stuck at the elegant curve of the stairs with one leg protruding through the wrought-iron banister while the men shove and swear. He rubs his chin absently. 'Do you think I should shave, Sophie?'

'If they haven't taken your shaving brush and razor.'

There's a sharp crack, indicating that the sideboard has suffered a precipitate drop in value, a clatter as the leg falls to the marble floor beneath, and some swearing from the bailiff's men.

'Well, I must look my best for my family, and—'

'Charlie, your family can go hang. What about me? Where am I to live?'

He ponders this. He, of course, is to be sent back to the country to cool his heels until he succeeds to his inheritance. 'We'll ask Bishop.'

'Oh, don't be ridiculous.' Dear, sweet Charlie, always so willing to think the best of people; when I consider the mistresses he could have chosen instead of me, I shudder. 'And, Charlie, I'm cheaper to keep than your horses. Everyone knows how expensive it is to stable horses in town.'

He scratches his chin. Stubble glows gold on it and I think with a pang that I shall never see it again – or at least that particular stubble on that particular face. 'You do have a lot of gowns, Sophie. And bonnets and gloves and whatnot.'

'Of course I do. I have to be fashionable. You wouldn't want some frump on your arm. And I'm not a truly extravagant woman. I didn't ask for my own carriage and equipage, did I?' I grab at one of the bailiff's men, descending the stairs with an armful of gowns. 'Wait, I bought some of those. Let me show you the receipts.' I rummage in my reticule.

'No point, miss, for we're taking them all.'

'That's Mrs Wallace, if you please.'

The man smirks and continues on his way.

'Charlie, he is taking my gowns! Stop him!'

Charlie smiles again, a ploy that has released him from many a tricky situation. 'My good man, must you take those?'

'Yes, sir, I am afraid I must.'

Charlie looks so woebegone – someone doesn't like him! – that I almost want to kiss him.

'My uncle's a very good sort of fellow,' he says apologetically.

'I thought you said he was a miserly old bugger.'

'Well, he's that too. How about my neckcloth, Sophie?'

I reach to retie it for him. I should make an admirable valet with my knowledge of gentlemen's clothing and buttons.

'Oh, Charlie.' I tuck the ends of the cravat inside his waistcoat. 'We were happy, weren't we?'

He blinks. 'Well, of course we were. You're a splendid girl, Sophie. Top-notch.'

It's as close to a declaration of love as he's ever come, apart from ludicrous things he's said in bed. His handsome face blurs as tears fill my eyes. 'I'll miss you.'

'I'll miss you, too.'

Just to make sure he will miss me as much as he should, I kiss him and he responds with his usual enthusiasm.

'Oh God, Sophie, have they taken the bed yet?' he groans into my ear, one hand hoisting up my skirts.

Two men, carrying chairs, snigger as they pass us. One calls down the stairs, 'The bedchamber's all but done, except for the bed, sir.'

I push Charlie's hand away. 'They can't take the bed. It's mine.'

'It'll take a good two hours to take apart, miss, but it must go,' the man replies, taking a good look at my exposed ankles.

'No. Absolutely not. It's mine, and the furnishings. I have the papers here.' I break away from Charlie and follow the two men downstairs. 'Where is Mr Bishop? I must speak with him.'

The hallway is crammed with furniture, statues, curtains, the silver tea service and the pretty china I chose. (Charlie chose the statues, most of which are of naked women.) We had a lot of possessions for our three rooms – dining room, drawing room and bedchamber on the first floor – and now we are losing them all, with Mr Bishop, arrived from the country today, to take charge of the disbursement of the furniture and of Charlie.

I know men, or so I like to think – but if I had, I would not have trusted Charlie so. I might have asked him about his seemingly bottomless pockets; I should have known. Now I see it as a quite ordinary kind of stupidity – two sorts of stupidity, to be exact: Charlie's carelessness with money and mine with my heart.

'Mrs Wallace, I presume.'

I spin around and dip a curtsy. 'Sir.'

Mr Bishop, who appears from behind one of the statues, is possibly a little younger than me – not so young as Charlie, of course – slight and fine-boned, a pair of gold spectacles perched on his nose. His hair is an uninteresting brown, his eyes dark grey and his coat appears a little too big for him. So this is the factotum of the ogre, the miserly old bugger, and I wonder how much of our conversation he has overheard. 'Sir, I must talk to you about my bed.'

Harry

This wicked seductress defies my expectations. I'd expected she would be a raddled tart of a certain age, and I had rather hoped that she had fled to her next protector and so I'd be spared the embarrassment of a meeting.

Mrs Wallace is, in fact, a rather slender, pretty young thing – older than Mr Charlie Fordham, of course, red-lipped (not entirely thanks to Nature, I suspect), with a mop of dark curls held in check with a red ribbon. At the moment she's somewhat damp around the eyes – I suspect she intends to appeal to my better nature, or, if her opening statement is any indication, my baser nature.

'If your business is concluded here, ma'am, may I call you a hackney carriage?'

She grins. 'No, you may call me Mrs Wallace. Beg pardon, Mr Bishop, it was a dreadful joke. The bed, sir. It is *my* bed. Here are the papers to prove it.'

She thrusts a crackling sheaf of papers at me, with an extravagant dangle of blood-red seals, and one slender finger inserted between the folded sheets. 'This is the spot, here. It is the part of the will where it says the late Lord Radding left it to me.'

I read the appropriate paragraph. Her finger rests on the page, creating an odd sort of intimacy. Sure enough, the ancient and wicked Lord Radding left his best bed to his mistress – younger than he by at least five decades – and all its appurtenances.

'It is a beautiful bed,' she says with a great deal of earnestness, and folds the will closed. 'Will you not come and see it?'

I am sure – fairly sure – she means nothing improper in her statement; besides, I need to speak to her to make sure that young Mr Fordham made her no foolish promises. 'Very well, ma'am.'

'Oh, capital, sir!' She skips – there is no other word for her agility and lightness of step – up the marble staircase, dodging a large clock as it is carried down.

She grasps Mr Fordham's hand. 'Come, we must show Mr Bishop my bed and decide what's to be done.'

Mr Fordham shuffles along behind her, sighing heavily.

I clear my throat to get his attention and whisper, 'Sir, I think it best if I speak to Mrs Wallace alone. Lord Shadderly needs to be sure she'll make no further claim on you.'

He nods and lets go her hand. For one moment she looks absolutely forlorn, but the moment passes and she disappears around the corner with a flutter of muslin.

I follow her.

I don't trust her an inch.

The bed is the only piece of furniture in the room, which is decorated otherwise with a few drifts of dust and what must be a garter, lying sad and abandoned on the bare floorboards. The bed is huge and ancient, its posts dark with age and carved with leaves and flowers, the hangings a dark red silk. A bed made for sin.

She trots up the wooden steps necessary to get into the behemoth, and arranges herself on the red coverlet, ankles prettily on display.

'Look, Mr Bishop, how beautiful the painting of the tester is!' She points above her head and pats the bed with the other hand, as though inviting me to join her.

I take a step forward and angle my head to catch a glimpse of cavorting fleshy gods and goddesses, protected inadequately by wisps of cloud and surrounded by beaming fat putti.

'Very fine. And when do you intend to move this bed out, Mrs Wallace?'

She rests on one elbow. 'They say Queen Elizabeth slept on it.'

'And you must sleep on it elsewhere, ma'am.'

She twirls a lock of hair around one finger. 'Regretfully at the moment I cannot afford to move the bed.'

'Until you have another protector, I suppose.'

'Precisely.' She smiles, not quite shamelessly, but as though this is all just business for her. I suppose it is. I don't like the idea of this woman skipping carelessly into the arms of the highest bidder; she looks too fresh and pretty.

'If you were my sister . . .' I begin.

'If I were your sister, sir, you would arrange for me to enter into a similar arrangement blessed by the Church; nay, a lesser arrangement, for I'd be trapped for life with nothing of my own, not even a bed such as this.' She pats the coverlet, this time as though caressing a favourite dog.

I walk across to the window and prop myself up on the sill, wanting to move as far as possible from her and the huge bed. 'Why, ma'am, you would have nothing but your honour.'

'And very nice for them that can afford honour, I say.'

I wonder what this woman's story, is, that she came to such a pass; and who, and where, Mr Wallace is, even if such a person exists. She is not repentant, she is not resorting to tears or threats; she is remarkably stoic – or giving that impression – about her plight.

'I quite loved Charlie,' she says, taking me aback even further.

'Indeed.'

'Oh, yes. But it's possible, Mr Bishop, to love someone who you know is not the right person for you. Are you married, sir?'

'No, ma'am, I am not.' The last thing I need is a philosophical discussion with this woman. Or is she eyeing me up as her next protector? 'I presume we can expect no unfortunate results of this liaison?'

'Oh, sir!' She looks quite shocked. 'Do you talk, sir, of babies? Unfortunate results, indeed.'

I ignore her. 'Well, are there?'

She looks me in the eye. 'No, sir. I have made sure of it.'

'I presume Mr Fordham owes you no money?'

'No, sir. He owes me nothing.'

'Very well. You'll remove that bed, Mrs Wallace, and I trust you will have no further commerce with Mr Fordham.'

She smiles. 'Of course, sir, although is that not up to Mr Fordham? He does achieve his majority in a few months, I believe.'

'I hope he has better judgement.'

She pouts and twirls a loose curl between her fingers. 'You are not very flattering, sir. I am a woman of good sense and, whatever you think of my profession, I have a sense of honour. He'd do better with me than anyone else, and I'd keep an eye on his accounts next time.'

'Mrs Wallace, I don't intend to flatter you. My instructions are to make sure that you will not come to Mr Fordham with any claims of a financial nature in future; in short, that you are out of his life. As for your honour, I think you will find the rest of society does not concur with your definition, so I advise you, ma'am, to find another profession.'

This room, with the looming great bed and its pretty

occupant, is becoming a trifle close for my tastes.

'Oh, an excellent idea, sir.' She beams at me. 'You know, I have always fancied the law. Or perhaps I should try for a commission in one of His Highness's more fashionable regiments? I should look well in an officer's uniform, I think.'

Of course I should be outraged by her frivolity. I should bow with outraged dignity and stride from the room. I should certainly not be thinking of Mrs Wallace's slender neck rising from a black gown, a horsehair wig atop her curls; or worse, flaunting a set of regimentals, tight-trousered as any shameless actress. Good God, the woman is impossible – and possibly more accomplished in her current profession than I had first thought.

'Or,' she continues, 'I could return to the stage. I was quite good.'

Good is not the word I would have chosen. I clear my throat. It sounds horrendously loud in the quiet room. 'Enough, Mrs Wallace. May I enquire as to the where-abouts of Mr Wallace?'

She raises one foot a few inches – the drapery of her gown slips from her ankles – and flexes her silk slipper. 'Since you apparently must enquire, sir, the late Captain Wallace is in hell, and I wish you godspeed there, too.'

In the blink of an eye we have travelled from (mostly) good-natured wrangling to downright animosity. She has the last word and we both know it.

I bow with all the courtesy I can muster. As I pass her, I catch a whisper of her perfume, sultry and intoxicating – and doubtless expensive and not yet paid for, I remind myself.

Mr Fordham, heaving sighs, lurks on the stairs.

'Come, Mr Fordham, you should leave now. I'll call you a hackney carriage. Your mother and sisters are most anxious to see you back at home.'

'But Sophie – you must help her move her bed, Bishop. She's a good-hearted girl.'

'Very well. You won't be bothered by Mrs Wallace again.' I take his arm.

His lip quivers. 'But I should *like* to be bothered by her.'

I bite back a sharp retort.

After I see Charles Fordham safely stowed in his hackney carriage I make haste to solve the problem of the bothersome Mrs Wallace and her bed.

Harry

I find Mrs Wallace sitting on a large, neatly folded pile of pillows, sheets and feather bed, the bed stripped to its mattress.

'I have arranged storage for your bed and temporary accommodation for you, Mrs Wallace, at Mr Fordham's request. A driver and a cart will arrive shortly.'

'That's very good of you, sir.' She proceeds to remove the mattress that lay beneath the feather bed and I move forward to help her. 'May I ask where?'

'At Bishop's Hotel.'

'Bishop's Hotel? Your family owns it?'

'They do, ma'am.'

She looks at me with a satirical smile. 'Oh, I know what you think. I assure you, I can be discreet. How very pleasant that you can visit your family!'

I'm annoyed that my misgivings show on my face and

am then surprised when she says with apparent sincerity, 'Oh, I beg your pardon.'

She unloops the rope that was the support of the mattress and coils it neatly. 'Is the man with the cart strong?'

I bristle with offended male pride. 'I assure you I am quite strong enough to deal with dismantling your bed, Mrs Wallace.'

'Oh, certainly.' She strolls over to the window and props herself against the window ledge. 'Pray proceed. The steps double as storage. You will find a mallet and a wedge there. There is not a single steel bolt or screw in the whole piece except for the curtain rails. It's very well made.'

I walk around the bed silently cursing myself for my arrogance. I am not sure that even the brawn of my brother-in-law Thomas Shilling, a huge ex-pugilist of some twenty stone of muscle, or even two of him, if they existed, could dismantle this monstrosity of fornication. I shall be like the minnow that swims alongside a whale. Grimly I unbutton my coat.

How many other men have unbuttoned their coats (and more) in the presence of Mrs Wallace and her bed?

I am spared further disturbing thoughts by the arrival of Thomas and his son Richard, a skinny beanpole of a fellow who is much the same size and dimensions as one of the bedposts. Richard stares entranced at Mrs Wallace who rewards him with a dazzling smile.

'Come along, lad,' Tom says to him. 'Look sharp, now. Harry, they're doing the fattened calf and all for you at the hotel; Mrs Bishop is airing the sheets for you and has the kitchen all in a tizzy. They're that excited to see you. Now, this bed. Well, now.'

He steps around it as though facing an opponent in the ring.

'Tester off first, Father, I reckon,' Richard says.

'One moment, gentlemen.' Mrs Wallace trips forward, beaming. 'If I may.' She runs up the steps again and stands on the frame of the bed, holding on to a post and reaching on to the tester. 'I had to take the precaution – if you would not mind catching these as I throw them down—'

Good God, she tosses down a half dozen bonnets, three gowns, a couple of shawls, and handfuls of stockings.

'They took some things I owned,' she explains, 'so I was careful to conceal the rest. Pray be careful with the flowers on that bonnet, Mr Bishop.'

'What shall we do with these, then, Uncle Harry?' Richard asks.

'Take them off!' I snap at him, for he sports a bonnet on his head, stockings festooned around his shoulders, and a silly grin on his face.

'We'll wrap the clothes in the curtains and I shall

carry the bonnets,' Mrs Wallace says. She looks down on us, laughing, standing on one foot like a tightrope dancer, and for a moment I smile back at her, as charming and pretty as she is.

But it's Tom who lumbers forward and offers his hand to her and she descends as gracefully as a queen while I feel like a fool, although I cannot say exactly why.

So the work begins in earnest. The tester, that amounts to a large painting in a wooden frame, sits atop a railing that runs around the bed, set on top of the bedposts. We lower it with some difficulty, for it is a large and unwieldy piece, and set it against the wall. Tom unfastens the rail that holds the curtains and Richard and I dart forward to become entangled with yards of brocade, from which we emerge sneezing, and which we fold under Mrs Wallace's guidance.

Thomas sets to work with the mallet and wedge, and Mrs Wallace runs to catch the wooden bolts in one of her bonnets. Richard and I meanwhile steady the solid pieces of wood as they loosen and sway and carry them to the side. Mrs Wallace chats to Thomas about his grandchildren and makes Richard blush by asking him if he has a sweetheart. Me she ignores, and I am not sure whether I'm thankful or resentful, but eventually the bed is reduced to a pile of lumber and brocade.

We take the first load downstairs to the cart and discover another impediment. Thomas has promised sixpence to a boy to hold the horse's head, and a small crowd of ne'er-do-wells and loungers has collected. The boy, a child of about six who attends his task with great pride, may prove inadequate to guarding the contents of the cart.

I suggest Richard stays and that I assist in carrying.

'Indeed no,' Thomas says. 'It's not right for a gentleman and carrying is what Richard is paid to do.'

'Oh, indeed!' Mrs Wallace pats a blushing Richard on the arm. 'You'd never think he was so strong!'

And so I find myself the guardian of the cart and subjected to loud and vulgar comments on my parentage and my private activities by the onlookers.

'Ignore them, Mr Bishop,' Mrs Wallace murmurs as she leaves with Thomas and Richard. 'They mean no harm.'

I am not convinced, although I suspect that the insults and crude comments are self-perpetuating, less to do with my appearance (employed, respectable) than with the desire to outdo each other in fantastic flights of the imagination. Indeed, I am quite impressed with the breadth and rich detail of the onlookers' speculations. I also notice that, for the most part, they fall silent and remove their hats when Mrs Wallace appears, only to renew their efforts with the greatest of vigour, as though refreshed by their silence, when she goes back into the house.

'Do I still get my sixpence, sir?' the child asks, as though the insults are part of his job and he resents a new recipient.

I assure him he does, and after several trips the bed is loaded and we are ready to depart. Before I think of doing so, Thomas offers his hand to Mrs Wallace, who alights gracefully on to the seat of the cart. Richard and I take our seats on the cart tail, our legs dangling. As we leave for Bishop's Hotel I raise my hat to the crowd, who respond with some huzzahs mixed in with the insults.

Sophie

So this Mr Bishop is connected with Bishop's Hotel! I am quite astonished, but then not so much. For all he looks like a gentleman, there are certain indications – his accent, the ill-fitting coat – that mark him as a servant, and of course my neighbours knew him for what he was immediately. An educated and gentlemanly servant, it is true, but someone who has ascended the slippery slope of social advancement on his own talent and wits. No wonder he is so nervous around me. He does not want to be associated with a woman of ill repute.

I have become great friends with Mr Shilling while Mr Bishop glowers and I flirted a little with Richard to make him glower more; but it was so easy I lost interest.

I am intrigued to find out why Mr Bishop is so unwilling to visit his family, and I am to find out soon enough.

I have never stayed at Bishop's Hotel for it is not the sort of place that Charlie and his friends and family would patronize, since it is neither fashionable, smart, nor conveniently located for the fashionable centre of London. Rather, it is a small, ramshackle, frowsty sort of place, frequented by shifty gentlemen awaiting the arrival of a banker's draft, salesmen selling noxious drafts and potions, and widows of dubious reputation; and although I am one of the latter myself I am fashionable, and would turn up my nose at the accommodation at Bishop's. Or at least in former times I would have done so. Now, my circumstances are changed.

We drive into the courtyard, where a carriage disgorges its occupants and ostlers unharness the horses. All is bustle and efficiency.

A smiling gentleman, prosperous in appearance with a fat gold watch chain, consults his watch, and hooks his thumbs into his waistcoat as the passengers step out and stretch and shake out travel-creased greatcoats or skirts. He greets a few, shaking some by the hand, and I notice he does so as an equal. He is an older version of Mr Harry Bishop, but more genial and more at ease in the world. A waiter holds a door open, bowing, to admit the passengers into the hotel.

But then a woman, dark-skinned and all brilliance

and colour in a sapphire-blue gown and rich cashmere shawl, runs to the foot of our cart.

'Harry! Lord, you should have given us more notice. Come here, then.'

To my great amusement she grabs Bishop and bestows a smacking kiss on him. He squirms away like a small boy. 'Ma'am! Not in front of everyone.'

How delightful to see Mr Bishop reduced to normal humanity! But she advances on me as Mr Shilling helps me down from the cart. 'Mrs Wallace, welcome to Bishop's Hotel.'

I curtsy and murmur a greeting.

Mrs Bishop sums me up in a glance. She knows who I am, she knows the value of my gown and bonnet, and quite likely she knows Charlie has cast me off. She is friendly but cautious and her shrewd gaze implies that she does not altogether trust me.

She turns her attention to the contents of the cart. 'A bed! Why, what a monstrous great old thing. Tom and Richard, if I may impose upon you to set it up for the lady—'

I am about to say it's not necessary, but her son starts to say something of the sort and I am compelled to disagree, and instead express my thanks at her kindness.

'You and I shall drink tea, Mrs Wallace,' Mrs Bishop says, and leads me inside the inn, along a passage and some twists and turns, up a few steps, around a corner, down a few steps, and into a comfortable parlour. From the sewing discarded on the sofa and a newspaper tossed on to the table, I guess it must be the private quarters of the Bishop family.

Mrs Bishop summons a maid to bring cups and saucers but makes tea herself from a kettle on the hearth and a tea caddy on the mantelpiece. When the maid has come and gone, and tea is poured, she sits back with a sigh, a busy woman enjoying the chance to sit and gossip for a while.

But Mrs Bishop does not gossip. She comes straight to the point. 'I know who you are, Mrs Wallace. I have something of a fondness for scandal magazines. I can't say I'm altogether comfortable with you under my roof but Harry insisted.'

'You need not worry, ma'am. This is a temporary measure only while I seek other employment.' She raises her eyebrows and I continue, 'I shall return to my father's theatre company.'

She chuckles. 'Very well. I beg only that you won't break my son's heart.'

Break Mr Bishop's heart? I'm not sure that loyal factotum has one. 'His heart is safe from me,' I say. Besides, simply put, the gentleman cannot afford me.

'Don't tell me you don't notice the way he looks at you,' she says. 'More tea, Mrs Wallace?'

'I assure you you're mistaken, Mrs Bishop.'

She shakes her head. 'I know my son. But I daresay your paths won't cross again. Ah, here's Mr Bishop.'

Sure enough, the senior Mr Bishop enters the room and bows to me and gives his wife a hearty kiss. 'Mrs Wallace, eh? Mrs Bishop's a great follower of yours. She went searching all over for trimmings for a bonnet like yours after she read about it in the paper.'

Mrs Wallace frowns but pours him a cup of tea. 'I am interested in fashion, my dear. Any woman is.'

'I've persuaded Harry to stay the night,' his father says. He pours his tea into his saucer and blows on it to cool it.

The parlour door opens. 'Harry, my dear, we were just saying you looked tired. And thin, too. Are you eating enough?'

Harry enters the parlour and looks surprised to see me there. 'Of course I am, ma'am.'

'We'll make sure you have a good dinner,' his mother cries. 'We'll have raisin pudding – it was his favourite when he was a child, Mrs Wallace. He would take all the raisins out and line them at the edge of the plate so he could save them for last because he liked them so much.'

'I managed to break myself of that habit a few years ago,' Harry says and at first I think he's absolutely serious. But no, astonishingly enough there's a glint of humour.

Mrs Bishop, however, is undeterred. She has me, a captive audience, and despite warning me off her son, she cannot resist the opportunity to boast about him. 'Fetch the pencil drawing, Harry, my dear.' She turns to me. 'We had an artist staying with us when Harry was a little scrap of a thing, and he was good enough to do some drawings of the children.'

'In lieu of paying his bill properly,' says Mr Bishop senior, bending to light a clay pipe at the fire.

'He will never let me forget!' cries Mrs Bishop. 'Over twenty years ago and still he complains. But I would not part with this picture for the world.'

Harry hands me a framed picture. It is a charming pencil sketch of a litter of children, for such is how they appear, all tumbled together, a mass of round cheeks and curls and mischievous eyes.

'I have never seen a lovelier infant than my Harry,' his doting mother says.

Harry rolls his eyes.

'What lovely children. Which one is he, ma'am?'

'Oh, it is as plain as the nose on your face!' Mrs Bishop leans over my shoulder and taps a finger on the glass. 'This one!'

'Why, so it is.' With the excessive lengths of curling hair and the dress I thought the child a girl. 'And the others, ma'am? What of them?'

Mrs Bishop is only too happy to regale me with tales

of Harry's brother and sisters, although I am over-whelmed by the flood of anecdotes and praise. I learn there is a brother at sea, a sister who is a housekeeper, another who married a chandler in Bristol, and the sister who is married to Mr Shilling the carrier and the mother of young Richard and three others.

'And you'll dine with us, ma'am?' Mr Bishop senior asks as his wife pauses for breath.

Harry looks horrified.

'That's most kind, sir, but I should not wish to intrude. I know you will want your son to yourselves. I beg you will excuse me.'

'We'll send a footboy with dinner to your room,' Mrs Bishop says. 'You can't eat in the taproom; it's not fitting.'

Harry

Good God, you would never think a whore graces the establishment. Yet my father, who had eyed her ankles the whole time – and very fine ankles they are too – makes much of what a polite young lady she was and how her manners matched those of the finest in the land, although I am not sure how he has come to this con-clusion. My experience has been that the higher the personage, the worse his or her manners are, particularly inside their house.

My mother raves in an equally idiotic way of her gown and bonnet and whether her presence will make Bishop's Hotel fashionable. 'But mind you, Harry,' she says out of the blue, 'you can't go falling in love with her. She's far above the likes of us.'

'Don't worry, Ma. I can't afford her.'

'What a thing to say!' my mother screeches. 'Shocking!'

'She's the lady in the fashion papers?' our waiter, napkin over his arm, rouses himself from picking his teeth at the sideboard.

'Attend to your business and stand up straight,' I instruct him. 'Yes, she is a woman of ill repute but regretfully her former protector could not afford to house her elsewhere.'

'Oh, we don't intend to charge her,' my father says. 'Maybe if a newspaper knew she were here—'

'Absolutely not!' I say.

My mother frowns. 'I don't think that is fitting, Mr Bishop. Surely you can tell the poor dear has a broken heart.'

'How, ma'am?'

'Oh, stop.' My mother swats at me with her napkin. 'She's a brave girl, but you men cannot know the suffering of a woman's heart.'

My father belches.

I'm tempted to do the same.

'Would you like me to look at the accounts, Pa?'

I lift a hair from the gravy on my plate.

He brightens. 'Would you, my boy? I've been having a bit of trouble.'

Oh no. What am I letting myself in for? I have long experience of my father's bits of trouble within the ledgers.

Several hours later numbers dance up and down columns, switch sides mysteriously, and blur in front of my eyes. I remove my glasses and rub my eyes.

'This is a mess, Pa.'

'Oh, lord. That bad? She won't give me a moment's peace.' My father relights his pipe, elbows on the kitchen table. By the hearth the kitchen boy sleeps on the flagstones, several of the cats curled up with him.

'Then let Ma keep the books.'

'I couldn't do that.'

I don't argue. I know from long experience it's hopeless. 'I think the cook is ordering extra butter and selling it. He's bought enough butter in the past month to float this hotel down the Thames in a sea of grease, yet there's precious little in the kitchen. You need an abacus, Pa. You keep making mistakes when you add.'

'Ten fingers are good enough for me, son. They were good enough for my old dad.'

'He was missing a thumb.'

'True, true.' He nods through blue clouds of smoke.

I blow on the ink in the ledger to dry it. I have solved some of the problems, but I know that once my father is let loose on it again mathematical chaos will reign once more.

Above our heads a bell clangs.

'Room sixteen,' my father says without bothering to glance at the row of bells. He knows the chime of each one the way others recognize voices. 'Mrs Wallace.'

'I'll go.'

I don't need a light for the stairs and corridors that I've trod all my life. The hotel is mostly quiet now, and I wonder what Mrs Wallace can require so late – although for her probably it is the time of night when parties and entertainments begin.

I tap at the door.

The door opens a crack and there she is, her face illuminated by a candle. 'Oh! Mr Bishop.'

'You expected someone else, ma'am?'

'I rather hoped it might be a female servant. But no matter. I can manage.'

Lewd thoughts of stays and stockings and other female mysteries dance through my mind.

'But never mind. Come in and drink a glass of wine with me.'

'Well, I . . .' I can hardly make the claim that Bishop's Hotel is a respectable establishment, since it really isn't; certainly it isn't one now.

'Come in.' She smiles and tugs at my sleeve. 'We got off on the wrong foot, Mr Bishop, and I want to let you know I'm not that bad.'

'I never said you were.'

'You didn't have to.' But she opens the door a little wider and I enter the bedchamber. In the shadows the huge bed looms.

A small table with the remains of dinner and a half-drunk bottle of wine stands in front of the fireplace that has burned down to a red glow.

'You have only the one wine glass,' I say. 'I'll go—'

'Oh, nonsense. We'll share. See, I shall drink from this side, and you from the other.' She refills the glass. 'To your health, sir.'

After she has drunk she hands me the glass and I'm sorely tempted to put my lips where hers were.

'I like Mr and Mrs Bishop,' she says.

'What!' The mortifying image of my father supping tea from his saucer and my mother talking on and on, recounting embarrassing episodes of my childhood, come into my mind.

She smiles. 'Oh, I know you didn't want to bring me here, but beggars can't be choosers, can they? If I'd known before what Charlie's family had planned, I'd not be at such a disadvantage. Look, Mr Bishop, I'll sell one of my gowns to repay you.'

'I assure you my employer can—'

'I know Charlie didn't have any money.'

'I insist. You owe me nothing, ma'am.'

'Thank you.' She bows her head. 'I thought the raisin pudding very fine.'

'Yes, it was.' I'm tongue tied. 'Well, I thank you for the wine, Mrs Wallace. I intend to leave early tomorrow so I should . . . I should . . .'

'Do you wear those spectacles all the time, Mr Bishop?'

'Yes, except when I'm in bed.'

She smiles and rises to her feet. She reaches for the spectacles and removes them.

Harry

A revelation! Oh, heavens, had I but known! The ecstasies of the night are beyond my wildest and most sensual dreams; the beauty of her form, the exquisite fragrance of her person; the sweetness of her limbs and the wonder of her lips! I am overcome! Now I know what all poetry, all music is about (with the exception of vulgar street ballads although I come to those with a new understanding)! Oh, goddess! Adored, divine being!

Sophie

For a first time I suppose he did not acquit himself too badly.

Sophie

A new profession. Bishop's words echo in my head.

I cannot saunter to a club and, over brandy and cards with my privileged friends, reveal that I am in need of a *position*, some gentlemanly sinecure without a hint of labour or trade. The possibilities for a female, particularly a female of middling origins and poor reputation, are dire. With a loan I could maybe start a shop; with luck, and some fabrication of references, I might take on a new identity as a genteel sort of servant. My experience of marriage is such that I do not wish to repeat it, even if I were to find a gentleman willing to take me on, and neither of the above professions open to a woman in my circumstances hold much appeal for me. Or there's the theatre again.

I spend the morning skulking in my bedchamber, avoiding the sharp-eyed Mrs Bishop who doubtless knows I have spent the night fornicating with her son (I am afraid she may thank me for it), before setting forth to pay a call in the fashionable part of town.

It is time to ask advice of an old friend.

'Mrs Wallace?' The butler's eyebrows perform a positive ballet of contempt, amusement, and innuendo. How provoking that he should read the gossip papers – I shall have to mention to the Countess that her servants are underemployed.

'Is her ladyship at home?' I peer past him into the glory of gilt and marble that adorns the Earl of Dachault's hall, wondering if I am ever to get any further inside.

'No, ma'am.'

'Then pray ask if she is at home to Mrs Wallace née Sophie Marsden.'

'Sophie Marsden,' he repeats.

I tap my foot. 'If you please. We were at school together. Why, the stories I could tell you . . .'

The butler looks alarmed but opens the door a little further. I gain a foothold on the elegant marble flagstones.

'Wait here, if you please, Mrs Wallace.'

I am left standing in an entryway that has the dimensions of a small church. Marble pillars stretch to a painted ceiling that makes the tester of my bed seem modest; gilt abounds, cherubs frolic, and a footman stands guard preventing my entry into paradise as surely as if he held a flaming sword.

Stately footsteps approach, echoing from the cavernous depths, and the butler makes his way towards me with a ponderous dignity. 'Her ladyship will receive you . . . ma'am.' There's just a moment's pause, enough to convey a whole universe of dismay and disapproval.

I bestow a smile upon him and the footman, who slowly turns a crimson that matches his livery. And then I follow the butler up the wide marble stairs, past portraits of solemn bewigged ladies and gentlemen, and, once we have reached the first floor, down an imposing gallery. The butler opens a door and shows me into a room furnished in the most fashionable style – everything restrained and classical, with light pouring in from tall windows. A pack of small dogs run towards me in an unrestrained and decidedly non-classical way, yipping loudly, tails wagging, while their owner, seated on the sofa, stares at me in amazement. 'Sophie,' she says. 'Is it truly you?'

It's Claire, Countess of Dachault, a little plumper than when I last saw her hanging from a bedroom window at Miss Lewisham's school fifteen years ago. She snaps her fingers and the dogs run back to her; Claire always liked others to do as they were told.

'My butler said you were here to blackmail me,' she adds, as a spaniel jumps into her lap.

I rise from my curtsy. She doesn't sound particularly friendly, but she has admitted me to her house, and that is a good sign, and I think, but I'm not sure, that she is joking about the blackmail. There is a lady beside her, who is not so fashionably dressed and who has a definite frown upon her face.

'How are you, Claire?' I ask, wondering if perhaps I push myself forward in using her Christian name. 'You're looking very well.'

I now realize the other woman is Lizzie, who promised to be friends with me for ever, but who now looks distinctly hostile.

'Who would have thought you were to become so fashionable!' Claire continues.

Not fashionable enough, or possibly a little too fashionable, to be invited to her ladyship's soirées, I think, but I keep that to myself. Claire continues to inspect me, and I her – I think I am marginally better dressed although she has a few major advantages, such as a roof over her head, a husband, and a title.

'You must have some tea,' Claire says. 'Do come and sit down. Never mind the dogs, they growl only for show. Now, tell me what you were to blackmail me about. Yes, Lizzie, what is it?'

'Excuse me.' Lizzie stands and walks past me out of the room, banging the door shut behind her.

Well.

'I think she's still cross that you never told us about the wedding night. You were supposed to, you know.'

'Oh. Was I?' I giggle. 'The Captain really didn't know what he was about. It was quite embarrassing and he went into a sulk when I laughed and got drunk. He got drunk, I mean, not me.'

Claire stirs the teapot. 'Oh, I had to tell Dachault what to do. Apparently his mother had given him some very odd advice about how to ensure a son would be conceived.'

'Really? What?'

'It involved a poultice on his – now, Sophie, you're not really going to blackmail me, are you?'

'Lord, no.' I accept a cup of tea from her. 'I just said that so the butler would admit me.'

'Well, of course I'm delighted to see you. But why, after all this time? Why, it must be fifteen years.'

I sip tea as I consider my answer. I could make a plea for the promise of eternal friendship we swore, but sooner or later I would have to admit that my motivation was rather more mercenary, or practical, to say the least. Besides, neither Claire nor Lizzie has made an attempt to see me in London – and Claire is high enough in the ton that she could consort with anyone, whatever their reputation. Lizzie, I seem to remember, married some sort of clergyman, and is probably more concerned with appearances.

So I decide to go straight to the point. 'I seek your ladyship's patronage.'

'My patronage? Why? I thought you did rather well with, ah, the patronage of gentlemen. Even Dachault says he couldn't afford you. Not that I'd let him, of course. I see to it that he keeps busy with the House.'

I don't want to tell her about Bishop and how his words intrude inconveniently upon my mind. Doubtless Claire knows about me and Charlie, for we have been seen together at fashionable spots and reported upon frequently in the press, as 'the notorious Mrs W—' and 'the juvenile Mr F—'.

'Claire, the truth of the matter is that I'm past my prime, and since marriage is out of the question, I must seek another profession.'

'Ah.' She smiles with great enthusiasm. I remember how Claire loved to concoct schemes – it was she, after all, who organized my elopement. She beckons to the footman who stands by the door.

For one horrible moment I wonder if she is about to have me thrown from the house, but instead she says, 'Peter, pray ask Mrs Buglegloss if she will join us. And fetch an onion from the kitchen.'

'How would milady like it prepared?'

'Peeled and raw,' she says. 'And hot water, too, we need more tea.'

Has she gone quite mad?

'You must repent,' she says after the footman has left, 'and Lizzie will do the rest.'

'But I don't feel like repenting. No one has asked Charlie to repent. Why should I? And Lizzie's married name is Buglegloss? That is ridiculous. And she clearly doesn't approve of me, Claire, so I should let her alone.'

She strokes a spaniel that has clambered on to her lap and gazes at her with adoring eyes. 'Lizzie is widowed and employed by me as my secretary. She has been most active in my work assisting gentlewomen in distressed circumstances – why, she was one herself.'

'Oh, I don't think so.' I wrinkle my nose. 'I'm not sure I'm a gentlewoman. Maybe I'd better go and see my father and beg for a role with his company.'

'As you wish,' Claire says in the maddening sort of way that means she expects me to do whatever I am told. 'A little remorse for your life of debauchery might make Lizzie more approachable. She can be such a stickler for good behaviour. You had best start acting.'

'Very well,' I say. 'But I am an *actress*. Why, pray, do you need an onion?'

She gives me a shrewd look. 'And when was the last time you were on the stage, Sophie?'

Regretfully, I enjoy the following scene immensely. The only drawback is that I am drenched in rosewater to cover the onion smell, and the dogs sneeze whenever they are near me.

Lizzie enters the drawing room to find me slumped on the sofa, with Claire posed in the act of offering me her vinaigrette.

'Why, she is quite overcome!' Claire says.

'Oh, I have been wicked, wicked,' I sob through onion-inspired tears.

The dogs, who seem to come to the decision that the comfort of the sofa is made unpalatable by the rosewater, run over to Lizzie to see if she smells better.

'What is this?' Lizzie asks with deep suspicion.

'You know of what we were speaking, Lizzie,' Claire says.

'Indeed?' As Lizzie speaks, I steal a glance at her through my tearing eyes. She stands almost as far away as the footman, which is just as well. Her arms are folded, an expression of perplexity on her face. It could be worse.

'How may I ever reclaim my lost honour?' I weep piteously. 'It is impossible.'

'Lizzie, we must help her!' Claire declaims.

'Yes, but . . .'

Accompanied by the dogs, Lizzie approaches. 'Oh, my dear Sophie, I am saddened by your plight. And to think that we encouraged you on your path to ruin by helping you to elope at such a tender age!'

A dog sneezes.

So does Lizzie. 'Phew, open a window. You're using an onion, aren't you?'

I discard the reeking vegetable and blow my nose. 'We never could fool you; I admit it, Lizzie. I'm afraid I don't really repent, but I don't want to be a courtesan any longer. I'm too old.'

Lizzie crosses to a desk and draws out a hefty quarto volume bound in leather, bursting with scraps of paper and with ribbons marking places. She and Claire pore over the book together. 'How about this one? No, that would never work. Sophie is far too pretty and his lordship has a wandering eye.'

'What are you talking about?' How typical of Claire and Lizzie, talking over my head when it is my fate to be decided.

'Can you sew a straight seam?' Lizzie asks. 'Do you like children?'

'Yes, of course I can; old Lewisham taught us. And no, not in general.'

The icy stares that meet me indicate that I have made a rash statement to two proud mothers. 'I have met some children whose company I enjoyed very much,' I add in a placatory way. 'You must understand that in my circles children are seen as an unfortunate accident, and in fact very few children are to be met with.'

'How dreadful,' Lizzie says.

'Surely you do not suggest I become a governess!' Despite the lingering effects of onion, I laugh uproariously.

'Have you read any books at all since leaving school?' Lizzie asks.

'Oh, lots. You spend rather a lot of time waiting around as a courtesan.'

'Pray do not elaborate,' Lizzie says, on her high horse once more.

'You always had very nice handwriting,' Claire says with approval. 'And you used to play the piano and sing very well.'

'I still do.' Although possibly not the sort of songs performed in the Countess of Dachault's drawing room.

'If you're to be a governess you'll need some good, plain gowns,' Lizzie says, looking at my plainest day gown with distaste. 'And you must keep your bosom covered. Perhaps one good gown, although not the one you're wearing, for it is far too revealing, in case you are asked to dine with the family. You must look respectable, Sophie.'

'And I think it best if she uses her maiden name, don't you, Lizzie?' Claire says.

'But I was married!' God knows I have no wish to honour the name of the late unlamented Captain Wallace, but it seems unfair to blot him out entirely.

'It does not seem entirely honest,' Lizzie says. 'But—'

'You shall be a widow,' Claire proclaims.

'I *am* a widow. I think.'

'Ah!' Claire snatches a letter from between the pages of the book. 'Here's one that would work. Lord Shadderly seeks a lady to accompany his ward to assemblies and events in the country and teach her music. Lady Shadderly, it seems, breeds frequently and has no interest in society.'

Lizzie frowns. 'Is the Viscount not a relative of your, er, Mr Fordham?'

'Pay no attention to that. It's a very obscure connection,' Claire says. 'I expect it was Beresford, the head of the family, who told Fordham to drop you. So it's not exactly a governess position, more of a companion. I think it would be excellent. They live in Norfolk.'

'I'm not sure . . .' It sounds dreadful. Some high-handed Viscount deciding he wants to push his illegitimate daughter up the social ladder, his wife sulking that he should put his by-blow before his legitimate children, and hours of country entertainment.

'Then it's all settled,' Claire says. 'I'll write a letter introducing you, Sophie. Let's have some wine. We should drink to Sophie's success.'

Lizzie, who seems to be softening a little, exchanges glances with me. Fifteen years may have passed but

Claire is still telling us what to do, Lizzie is our conscience, and I— I don't even know that this is what I want. I'm delighted to be back in the company of my dear friends but setting myself up as some sort of bastion of respectability in the country (mud! Cows!) does not sit well with me.

Sophie

When I leave the Countess's house I instruct the driver of the hackney carriage to take me to the theatre where my father's company played last, when they did a pantomine at Easter. Not a particularly successful engagement, following some unpleasantness with actresses and my father's roving eye, it was at a run-down theatre in the same unfashionable area as Bishop's Hotel. Despite its impressive name, the Royalty Theatre is decidedly plebeian in nature.

'Oh, yes, ma'am, left weeks ago,' the doorkeeper informs me. He removes his pipe from between yellowed teeth and pokes at its contents with the stub of a pencil.

I smile brightly and inwardly curse my improvident parent for not sending me word. On the other hand I have not seen him for six months, since I wanted to keep Charlie away from actresses other than myself.

'Mr Sloven's inside. He's rented the theatre for the

summer.' The doorkeeper replaces the pipe in his mouth and puffs out a pungent cloud of smoke.

Jake Sloven! The manager who is notorious among actresses for developing half a dozen extra hands and for conducting auditions in a horizontal position.

'Good heavens, is that the time? Pray give my regards to Mr Sloven.'

'Not so fast,' booms Jake Sloven who has appeared behind the doorkeeper. He sports a napkin and grease stains; eating is his other interest in life. 'Why, Sophie Wallace, my dear! I heard your young man threw you over.'

'Mr Sloven, I regret I—' But the stage door swings open and I am hauled inside by Sloven, who takes a good leisurely look down my bosom, plants another hand on my arse, and manages to rub his grease-scented body against me all in one dexterous move.

'But you must read for me, my dear. Why, your dear papa said to me only a few days before he left town, "You must look out for my little Sophie. There's no one who sings and dances quite like her, and her voice! She can whisper from the back of the stage and make them weep in the gallery!" '

'How charming.' I dodge the thick arm around my waist and another snakes out to capture me.

'How about a kiss for your old friend? Why, I feel almost like another father to you, my dear.'

This is disturbing for so many excellent reasons that I am dumbstruck. 'Do you know where my father is, sir?'

'Up north. No, he said Bath and Bristol, I think . . .' he leers into my bosom to refresh his memory. 'Or did he mention Bury St Edmunds?'

His lips descend to my face. He has had onions for dinner, it seems.

'Goodness!' I drop my reticule and duck, a dire mistake as I find when he assists me to an upright position. 'Why, certainly I'll read for you. What would you like to hear?'

By this time, in a ballet of gropes and evasion, we have reached the stage.

'In my office,' he says, breathing heavily.

'Oh, no. Here, surely. There will be more room for me to dance.' I swish my skirts and he breathes heavily at the sight of my ankles and licks his lips as I remove my bonnet.

Foolishly I let him choose the play and he thrusts a playbook of *Othello* at me.

'Fair Desdemona.' He removes the napkin from his waistcoat and dabs his thick lips. 'And I shall play Othello.'

There is a sofa on the stage. Well, of course there would be. The noble Moor hitches at his breeches and gestures to me to recline.

'Should I not be praying?' I'm not sure I want to be

on my knees in front of Jake Sloven – at least, I had not intended to assume the position so early – and it crosses my mind that I should run out screaming. But I am an actress! There is no reason why Sloven should not hire me (and doubtless he has dozens of prettier women in his employ).

I outwit him by standing with my palms together, eyes raised heavenward. Of course this way I cannot see what he is about – for a large man, he moves quietly (from long practice) – and I shriek as pudgy hands land on my hips and I drop my playbook.

'*Down, strumpet!*' he trumpets in my ear.

I fall to my knees and scrabble for the playbook, bringing myself on a level with the fall of his breeches, and it is not a pleasant sight, gravy stains and straining buttons. Having found my place again, I respond with throbbing pathos, '*Kill me tomorrow: let me live tonight!*'

'*Nay if you strive—*' Othello strives to get his hand into my bosom.

'*But half an hour!*' I must be the only Desdemona who wishes the scene to last but half a minute.

Sloven hauls me to my feet, a firm grip on bosom and thigh. '*Being done, there is no pause.*'

And there certainly is not. I scramble to my feet and run around the couch. '*But while I say one prayer!*'

Sloven lumbers after me, breathing heavily with the effort. I grab a pedestal, a good two-foot length of sturdy wood painted to look like marble, and thrust it in his direction.

'It is too late!' Sloven says with gusto, but not as Shakespeare intended, tossing his playbook aside and bearing me on to the couch, hoisting my skirts.

I swing the pedestal and it meets the side of his head with a loud thud.

He drops like a stone on to the couch that cracks beneath his weight, and slowly subsides to the floor in a ruin of gilt wood and velvet. Blood spreads in a dark pool on the floorboards.

I stand shocked and out of breath. Is he dead? He is certainly unconscious. I do not want to investigate lest he rear to life and ravish me on the floor in revenge.

Why have I been such a ninny? This is not the first time I have had to fight off an amorous manager. Why did I not flirt and smile and tease a little instead of taking Sloven as a serious threat to my (somewhat threadbare) virtue? I am an actress. This is how business is done. Sloven is a lecherous brute, but I knew that.

The pedestal falls to the floor and I am aware of how very quiet the theatre is.

Oh, God. I am undone. I am a murderess. I retrieve my bonnet with shaking hands and tie the ribbons as I run for the stage door.

'Mr Sloven has had an accident,' I babble to the doorman, who has fallen into a peaceful slumber and comes awake with a start, spilling ash from his pipe down his waistcoat. 'Please assist him.'

I wave down a hackney carriage and collapse on to the seat. I must leave London. I shall stay at Bishop's Hotel, keeping quietly to my room, and accept the position as the governess-companion (mud! Cows! How I welcome them!) and become a new and virtuous person.

My plan of meditating alone upon my newly minted character as a murderess and my usual one of a corrupter of honest men, both of which I long to reform, is foiled by the mother of the honest man I most recently debauched, Mrs Bishop.

She catches me when I come downstairs later that day with a note I have written for Claire, expressing my extreme thanks and my great interest in the governess-companion position. I even gritted my teeth and added my affectionate regards to Lizzie.

'Why, Mrs Wallace! You wish to send a letter?' She plucks it from my hand and peruses the name and address. 'Oh, certainly! I shall send one of the boys to the Countess of Dachault's immediately. And you must take tea with me.'

She grasps my arm in a way that reminds me uncomfortably of that of a Bow Street Runner making an arrest and escorts me into her sitting room. After she has brewed and poured tea, she looks at me expectantly, and

I oblige with a description of the Countess of Dachault's house.

' 'Tis a pity Harry did not have the chance to bid you farewell,' she says, pouring tea. 'He left for the country very early this morning. He has a brand-new position as house steward, you know. And he is doing remarkably well when you consider that he became a butler only three years ago when he was three and twenty. All say he is a clever and most capable young man, and not only his proud mother – why, Mr Bishop, do you wish for tea or shall I send for some ale?'

Mr Bishop senior, wearing his long linen apron, settles on the chair opposite mine where he can resume the perusal of my ankles and accepts tea.

I am much relieved to hear that Harry Bishop has gone back to the country, although somewhat horrified to find him younger than myself. I had not seen him since I fell asleep early this morning, exhausted by the gentleman's vigorous efforts.

'Mrs Wallace was just saying how this parlour reminds her of the Countess of Dachault's drawing room,' Mrs Bishop says to her husband.

'Indeed?' Mr Bishop, too, looks impressed by my boldfaced lie.

'Indeed, yes. Elegance and fashion combined with comfort,' I babble.

'Well now!' Mr Bishop takes a slurp of tea. 'We had

the Earl of Edminster's drawing room in mind, you know, for we were both in service there. I was his lordship's butler for some ten years and Mrs Bishop—'

She frowns at him and he clears his throat. Sensing that a change of subject is necessary I ask if they have attended the theatre recently. They are happy to chat of plays they have seen and I wonder that they are ashamed that once they were in service when they are so obviously proud of their son's position. Now and again I catch Mrs Bishop's speculative gaze, but so long as she does not turn on me and accuse me of being a shameless trollop who shall darken her establishment's door no longer, I am content. Besides, having seen some of the other inhabitants of Bishop's Hotel, I think myself an average sort of guest.

I am, however, the only one to have breached Mr Harry Bishop's virtue, through a compulsion I still do not understand and do not wish to dwell upon. Besides, I have much to do in the next few days, for I must sell my best gowns and find replacements of a dowdy, respectable sort that are not being sold because the original owner died of a hideous complaint.

Three days later I receive a letter saying that the position is mine and to my relief the newspapers do not report the sudden and violent death of Mr Jake Sloven.

I wish I did not dream of it so, of his blood spreading over the floorboards of the stage.

Harry

'The clouds,' Lord Shad says. 'Look at those clouds, Bishop.' He reins in his horse and rests a hand on the pommel of his saddle to examine the skies.

'Very fine, milord.'

'Like a cathedral.'

The cathedral spatters down a little rain.

Lord Shad's interest in clouds does not derive from his days as a Navy man. Rather, his innate gentleness expresses himself in a love for his family and a hobby of painting landscapes. His delicate, spare watercolours are hung throughout the house. Lady Shad, whom I first and mistakenly complimented on these efforts, laughed uproariously and said she barely knew one end of a paintbrush from the other.

But I see what he means. The sky is huge here because the land is so flat, and clouds change constantly with the wind from the sea, a half-day's journey hence. Grass in the meadows bends and flutters and nearby a heron launches itself aloft with cumbersome dignity. The land is criss-crossed with ditches and small canals and every house and cottage possesses an outside door on its first floor, a sober reminder that given an unfortunate combination of tides and winds, the waters may rise.

Lord Shad has told me of the last great flood here,

some twenty years ago, shortly before he went to sea, and which he found a great adventure, although several tenants had died and the flood had caused much destruction of crops and property. 'They blamed it on the late Viscount, my father,' he said. 'Folk round here think he was in league with the devil.'

I'd heard plenty of kitchen gossip about the wicked old Viscount and his many sins and cruelties. By all accounts, the Viscount's eldest son, who held the title for a short time before an untimely and unlamented death, was not much better.

'We must return.' Lord Shad straightens in the saddle and eases his bay mare around. 'I promised Charlotte I'd drink tea with her and the companion we've hired for Amelia. I believe she should be here by now.'

In very few households would the master invite a servant to ride with him purely for the pleasure of his company. I have a few duties relating to the estate – Lord Shad does not keep a land agent, but prefers to oversee such things himself. Once Parliament is in session at the end of summer and he spends more time in London, however, he plans to delegate more of the estate business to me. So we amble around his land on horseback, he gazing at clouds and occasionally throwing out the odd comment on his livestock and tenants.

'Have you any thought of marrying, Bishop?'

I inadvertently jerk the reins and the grey gelding on

which I am mounted breaks into a trot. Did I return from London with some sort of wild hunger in my eyes?

I rein my mount in. 'No, my lord.'

'If I may speak plainly, it would be appropriate for a man in your position. But I should warn you not to look to my ward.'

'But— but she's only sixteen!' And beautiful, although I do not think it tactful to say so; furthermore, a match between milord's illegitimate daughter and a house steward, even one of humble origins, would be no bad thing.

'Precisely. She's too young,' Lord Shad says, 'and I wish her to see some society before she considers any offers. On the other hand, I've found women pretty much get what they want, so if she sets her cap at you, Bishop, good luck to you.'

'I assure you, my lord, I've no intentions towards Miss Amelia, and I believe she's indifferent to me.'

'Very well, then. We'll speak no more of it.' He smiles at me with exceeding sweetness, awkwardness averted, and then his eyes brighten as he sees a trap approach. He raises his hat in salute. 'Talk of the devil.'

Miss Amelia and her brother John, Lord Shad's two wards, are driver and passenger respectively. They are ludicrously like his lordship in appearance, with the same sharp cheekbones and finely arched brows beneath dark hair, but how Miss Amelia manages to turn this into ethereal beauty and Master John, at twelve, appears mainly a dishevelled mass of long limbs, is a great mystery.

'Sir!' John cries to his guardian. 'Amelia will not let me drive. It's not *fair*.'

She elbows him. 'Manners. Uncle, sir, I trust you've enjoyed your ride. And I shall not let John drive, Uncle, for I don't want to end in the ditch.'

Her brother glowers at her, lower lip thrust out. She cuffs him in a friendly sort of way and we proceed to the house.

Diary of Miss Amelia Price

I don't know why the decision to keep a diary is such a troublesome thing. You start off full of good intentions and then, after a few days writing about the weather, become bored to death. And the decision when to write it is problematic. For instance, if I write in the morning as I do now, it is a convenient time but does not allow for the fact that interesting things may happen later and when I come to write about them I may have forgotten pertinent facts.

For instance, if I met a gentleman (fairly unlikely since we see little society).

I wonder if I should practise falling in love with Mr Bishop? He is quite handsome and gentlemanly.

But Aunt Shad said he had all the symptoms of a man attached to another. I do not know why she thinks so, for her attempts to find out – asking whether he has a sweetheart last night at dinner while the footmen sniggered and then requesting he pass the fish pie – met with little other than a polite smile and a shake of the head.

Later today while dressing for dinner:

Mrs Marsden is most charming and ladylike but I wonder why she travels with her own bed? And Mr Bishop was most put out about it. I suppose it interrupts the footmen's work.

7

Harry

This is a nightmare.

At first I think debauchery has addled my brain.

The hall of the house is littered and defiled with huge pieces of timber and swathes of embroidered bed hangings. They are familiar to me. I have seen the deities above smile on my efforts (somewhat blurred without my spectacles) and I have grasped the bedposts during the most intimate of activities. This is, in short, the bed I never thought to see again and owned by a woman who has no business in this house.

'My lord, I must speak to you most urgently—'

'Later, Bishop. Good God!' says Lord Shad. 'Did she not think we'd provide a bed for her? It is a bed, is it not?'

'I believe so.' I turn to one of our footmen who lingers, staring at the mess. 'Why is this here, Mark?'

'Sorry, Mr Bishop. You see, we must move the bed

that is in the young lady's bedchamber out first, and so . . .' He shrugs and with his hook stirs the pile of timber.

'Excellent workmanship. I don't think I've seen such fine wood carving since on board ship,' Lord Shad says. He examines one of the bedposts. 'Look here, John, does not this remind you of the carvings in Ely Cathedral?'

His ward squats to examine the carving more closely. 'Excellent, sir, there's a fox among the grapevines. And here, lilies and apples.'

'You will see, my lord, that the carvings are based on the book of the Song of Solomon,' says a familiar voice.

The voice is familiar, but the woman who descends the staircase is transformed. The riotous black curls are tamed beneath a cap and her gown and spencer reveal barely a hint of bosom. She is all modesty, correctness, and ladylike charm.

She curtsies to Lord Shad, who introduces her to his two wards and then to me. She allows me a polite smile and curtsy as though I am a total stranger.

John bows, gazing at her with awe, and she smiles sweetly at him before turning to his sister and taking her hands. 'Why, Lord Shadderly did not tell me what a lovely young lady you are. And so tall! But Lady Shadderly mentions that you sing and like music. We must find some to play together, for she said she is sadly out of practice.'

The two of them walk away, arm in arm and deep in conversation.

'She's so pretty!' John exclaims and blushes deep red.

'So she is.' Lord Shad gazes after the female wolf in sheep's clothing. 'But I am afraid you are stuck with the Reverend Dimmock for your lessons.'

'It's no fun without Amelia there,' John says as we enter the drawing room. 'I still don't see why she can't go to lessons with me.'

'Curate Dibble,' Lady Shad says. She sits with the infant Harriet at her breast on the sofa.

'What has Curate Dibble done?' Amelia asks.

Lord and Lady Shad exchange glances, while Mrs Marsden (*Mrs Marsden*) assumes the duties of pouring tea. Does her hand tremble as she passes me my cup? Mine does as I receive it.

'Curate Dibble,' Lord Shad says as he stirs his tea, 'wrote you an amorous poem in Latin that John found inside his copy of Suetonius. It was most improper. Fortunately you did not see it and John did not understand it.'

'Oh, yes I did, sir, even though he made some grammatical errors.' John blushes. 'I translated it for you.'

Amelia makes a face. 'Curate Dibble? He looks like a fish with those big blubbery lips. And I don't believe he's ever said a word to me.'

The infant disengages herself from her mother's

breast with a loud popping sound and Lady Shad reaches
for a slice of bread and butter. 'I doubt the Curate meant
to debauch her, my dear.'

'Then he should have addressed her as an honest
man,' Lord Shad says. 'You're dropping crumbs on to the
child's head.'

'And what if Miss Price has an overwhelming desire
to study the Classics?' Mrs Marsden enquires. 'I regret I
am sadly lacking in Greek and Latin.'

'John can teach her. It will do him good,' Lord Shad
says.

'No one ever asked me if I wanted to study Greek and
Latin,' Amelia says. 'I don't quite know why I should
need them, or, for that matter, why John should, although
apparently gentlemen need them to pursue a profession.
But I liked to keep John company.'

She looks troubled. She may sit in the drawing room
but her status, and that of her brother's, in the house
is uncertain. She has youth and beauty, she has pin
money from her position, a sinecure as poultry maid, and
although ostensibly she is the daughter of the coachman
Mr and Mrs Price and his wife, everyone knows she is
illegitimate and whose daughter she is. A marriage to a
curate or an upper servant such as myself is about all she
can hope for unless Lord Shad settles some money on
her. As for a profession . . . I remember my pompous
advice to Sophie and try not to squirm.

'What do you think, Bishop?' Lord Shad asks me.

'I beg your pardon?'

'I asked you what you thought of learning for women.'

This must be my chance to atone although how I can do so without blushing or making an utter fool of myself (or worse, revealing myself as a great hypocrite) is beyond me. 'I am in favour of it, my lord. My mother tells me that learning to read and write was the making of her and raised her in the world. But she could do so only because it was her father's whim to see his daughter educated, not because it was her right or her wish.'

'Your grandfather sounds like a remarkable man,' Lord Shad comments. 'He was a man of learning, himself?'

'He was of high birth. My mother's mother was his property.' In my bid for atonement I have revealed the shameful secrets of my family and my origins.

A silence falls, broken by Lady Shad's strange mixture of kindness and clumsiness. 'Bishop, will you take this child? I wish to drink tea.' She hands over Harriet and examines me frankly. 'You don't look black.'

Harriet blows a bubble at me as I receive her sweet weight in my arms. 'I resemble my father, ma'am.'

'Well, then. You know, Bishop, it's high time you got some of those yourself. Babies, I mean. They probably wouldn't all be black.'

'Ma'am,' Lord Shad interjects, 'leave the man alone,

and for God's sake stop speculating on his unbegotten offspring. Have you no sense of propriety?'

'Very little, Shad, as you should know by now. I was thinking of the kitchen cats. We used to have a ginger tom who would perch on top of doors so he could better drop on to our heads and terrorize us, but not all of his kittens were ginger. So I thought that Bishop's—'

'But my mother is no bluestocking.' I interrupt Lady Shad's assessment of me as some sort of stud animal. 'She cannot keep accounts, and she reads only the fashion papers, but she has great determination and energy and sense. I attribute that to the discipline of education.'

'I didn't offend you, I hope.' Lady Shad lays a hand on my arm.

'Not much, ma'am.' We smile at each other.

Harriet, in the crook of my arm, releases a large belch.

'I don't want to make an absolute fool of myself calling out my house steward,' Lord Shad comments. 'Pray leave him alone, ma'am.' He turns to Mrs Marsden (for so I must think of her now, or for at least as long as she's in the house, which hopefully will not be more than an hour or so) and says, to my horror, 'Bishop is on somewhat intimate terms with Lady Shad. He delivered our daughter.'

'He fainted,' Lady Shad says, nudging me.

Oh God.

Sophie

I know Bishop will reveal my secret. I know he suspects I followed him here for some purpose, and I wish I had had the foresight to ask his mother where he was in service. (But if I had done so, would she not have assumed I was in pursuit of him?)

I sit in the shabby drawing room and although I have been in the house less than one hour, I do not want to leave. I like this family – the children are charming and Lord Shad kindly. And I very much like Lady Shad, who for all her bluntness and indiscretion has good sense and a ready wit, and beauty too, although she does not strike me as a woman who cares overmuch for her appearance. Together they are delightful; surely this was a love match, and yet despite three children and his frequent absences in London, their affection seems undimmed.

To my surprise, Amelia is no country clod. She is modest and charming and I hope her singing voice is as sweet as her speaking voice.

I shall not leave. I am aware of Bishop's discomfort, how he tries to catch his employer's eye. I find myself admiring him a little for his confession, and for his praise of his mother, and intrigued by the idea of him as a man midwife. I suspect he is a little in love with Lady Shad – certainly they seem most comfortable with each other, she even nursing her child with him present – and that Lord Shad is aware of it too.

Harry places his cup and saucer on the small table with the other tea things. He clears his throat and stands, and so do I, ready to defend myself.

'If you'll excuse me, my lord,' he says. 'I—'

'Of course, you must see Mrs Marsden settled in. You'll both dine with us, if you please.'

Harry's back is stiff as he walks to the drawing room door and opens it. I bow my head in acknowledgement and smile at him.

Once we are outside we turn on each other like a pair of dogs about to fight.

'Why the devil did you come here?' he says.

'I was offered this position through the services of the Countess of Dachault.'

He looks unimpressed. 'You must leave immediately.'

'Certainly not.'

'You're under an assumed name. Is that the action of an honest woman?'

I shrug. 'It's my maiden name so there's little false about it.'

'Ma'am, you should not be here. It's not decent. Do you really think Lord Shad would welcome the former scandalous Mrs Wallace into his house?'

'No sir, but I consider I played that part. Now I play a different part, and remember, it was you who suggested

I change professions. So I have done. I have as much right as you to be here, sir.'

We have crossed the hall and now ascend the staircase.

'Why are you coming with me?' I ask.

'I shall instruct my footmen to disassemble that wretched bed, ma'am, for you must leave this house.'

'That is not very honourable.'

'If I were to take the honourable path, ma'am, I should leave this house myself.' The misery on his face takes my breath away.

'You may do so if you wish, sir. But the only person who can tell me to leave is Lord Shad, and if I find you have told him of my past, I will tell him that you debauched me in London, taking a most ungentlemanly advantage of your position at the hotel.'

'What!'

We are at the top of the stairs now and I fear we may both tumble down together as we come to a violent stop.

We both glare at each other and I am strongly tempted to slap him.

'Ma'am— I— you— that is— *you* debauched *me!*'

'Oh, certainly. And I may also mention that you harbour a *tendresse* for Lady Shad. She's a very lovely woman; I should not blame you one bit for it. Her husband may jest about it, but if I were a man I should not care to cross Lord Shad.'

'Enough.' He turns away and marches towards my bedchamber. I follow a little more slowly.

'What, not finished yet? Come, Matthew, look lively, man. The piece you have in your hand does not fit there, Mark, it's as clear as the nose on your face. We serve dinner in an hour and you have yet to change into your livery . . .'

It seems I am to stay. But I have to confess it is a hollow victory.

The next morning Amelia and I are to begin our lessons, but first she takes me to meet her parents, the coachman and his wife, Mr and Mrs Price. There is much affection between them and pride that their daughter has risen in the world, and their other child, John, sees fit to do the same. They have a third child of about six, a pretty fair-haired girl named Emma. Surely she cannot be yet another of Lord Shad's by-blows? She looks nothing like the others, but I remember Lady Shad's example of the ginger tomcat. I am surprised that Lord Shad has reformed so thoroughly; I could see that although he looked upon me with appreciation (even such a dowd as I am now) there is only one woman for him and that is his wife.

'But we must see the poultry and collect the eggs!' Amelia cries. She dons an apron and a wide-brimmed straw hat and, basket in hand, takes me outside. 'Do you like chickens, Mrs Marsden?'

'I like to eat them,' I say.

'They are very silly creatures.' She unlatches a gate to an enclosure where a variety of fowl roam and peck.

A goose rushes at us, wings out and hissing.

I shriek.

'He can't hurt you. Stop it, Oberon!' She flaps her apron at the creature and it runs off.

With great pride she introduces me to the poultry. My head reels with their Shakespearian names – there is a cockerel as aggressive as Oberon named Titus Andronicus whose neck she threatens to wring. Hens run over my feet and peck at the laces of my boots, thinking they are worms. They have a wooden enclosure and a trough full of hay, and Amelia invites me to push nesting hens aside to take their eggs. Their bodies are warm and soft and they make soft crooning sounds that remind me of the infant Harriet.

Ducks swim in and waddle around a muddy pool, and Amelia searches for more eggs. Ducks, she assures me, are far more clever than chickens, although I suspect they are clever at being ducks and that is all.

'So you are an admirer of Shakespeare,' I comment, after having been introduced to her best layer, Portia, and a duck matriarch called Juliet.

'Oh, yes. It is my greatest wish to appear on the stage.'

I wonder what Lord Shad will think of that.

'Are you by any chance related to Mr Marsden, the theatre manager? His touring company visited here last summer. It was quite splendid.'

Now I have learned that lies are best if you stick close to the truth, so I reply that yes, indeed, Mr Marsden is a relative, but go into few details. It is not widely known that the scandalous Mrs Wallace is the daughter of that gentleman, but I shall take no chances.

'It is a hazardous profession,' I tell her. Hazardous indeed; she might well find herself fighting off an amorous Othello. 'Certainly not one for a lady.'

'But, Mrs Marsden—' she pauses in counting the eggs in her basket. 'I am not a lady, nor can I become one. The position of poultrymaid is a kindness for which I am most grateful, for I am paid by the kitchen for eggs and fowl. But I am not sure I wish to do this all my life and be a dependant on Uncle Shad. Possibly I may marry, but I cannot count on it. Do you think I should marry Mr Bishop?'

'Mr Bishop? Has your— I mean, Lord Shad – has he suggested you should?' For some reason this makes me extremely uneasy.

'Oh, no. But Mr Bishop is here, and he is a real person.'

'Both those factors are certainly in the gentleman's favour,' I say.

'You see, I should really like to marry Benedict in

Much Ado About Nothing. Or Henry the Fifth. Not Hamlet, for he is too melancholy. I should not like to marry a gentleman who spends so much time talking about himself.' We walk back towards the house, she with her basket of eggs, while we discuss the merits of various heroes from Shakespeare as husbands.

'Mrs Marsden, forgive me for asking, but were you ever on the stage yourself?'

I could kick myself for revealing myself so. 'Only in a very few amateur productions. It was all very genteel.'

'So Mr Marsden never invited you to perform?'

'He is a very distant sort of relative.' Despite our proximity to the fowl, no cock crows as I deny my fond if absent sire.

Fortunately at this point we have entered the kitchen and I am spared having to tangle myself further as some sort of crisis seems to have occurred, with the cook and Harry Bishop facing off on opposite sides of the kitchen table while the staff gather around, wide-eyed and awed, like children watching their parents quarrel.

A large iron pot stands on the table and this is the cause of their disagreement.

'I assure you, Mr Bishop, this is how it is done in this household. Mr Roberts never had cause to interfere.'

'Maggots!' Harry reaches into the pot and flicks something on to the floor that wriggles until he steps on it. 'This will not do, ma'am.'

'His lordship is used to food from foreign parts.'

'Even in foreign parts, ma'am, they do not eat rotting food.'

'Indeed they do, sir. It is why they add spices.' The contempt and horror on the cook's face demonstrate that maggots represent all that is good about England, whereas spices are the horrid epitome of the foreign sensibility.

'I must disagree. They add spices because they like them.'

'Impossible!'

'And how many times have you served meat crawling with maggots to the family? It is a wonder they are still alive. Consider, ma'am, you may end up on the gallows. Would you serve such to downstairs?'

Her face expresses eloquently that she would serve the maggots without the meat to him and her grip tightens on her wooden spoon.

Harry nods to one of the footmen. 'Take this out. Give it to the pigs.'

The footman sidles forward, keeping a close eye on the cook as though she may spring to the rescue of the meat, and takes the pot. A sour odour arises from its depths.

'Well, *I* shan't be held responsible for a half-empty table,' the cook says.

'Roast chicken,' Amelia says and darts out of the door. After a very short time she returns with two limp corpses that she tosses on to the table. This girl, who petted and played with her fowl as though they were kittens, is entirely dry-eyed. 'Rosencrantz and Guildenstern. I never much liked these two,' she says. 'I thought sooner or later we should eat them.'

'Lord Shad will be expecting roast beef,' the cook says as though inviting someone to slaughter a cow instead, but a moment later she is snapping at one of the maids to put on a pot of water so they may pluck the birds. She shoots spiteful glances at Harry all the while. It is only too obvious she would prefer to plunge him into the boiling water.

'Miss Amelia. Mrs Marsden.' Harry makes a half-bow in our direction. 'May I be of assistance?'

'I wanted to show Mrs Marsden the kitchen,' Amelia says, oblivious of the hidden message that I certainly shouldn't be trespassing upon Harry Bishop's sphere of influence.

'Certainly you may show her the stillroom and laundry room too,' he says. 'I am sure Mrs Marsden is very interested in household management. And don't forget the brewhouse and icehouse.'

Amelia looks from me to him, puzzled by his tone, but I thank him effusively for being allowed to visit the kitchen and pour on a little exaggerated praise about what a well-run and clean place it is. The cook swells with pride and Harry frowns.

I escape with Amelia as soon as we can, trying not to wonder why I think of Mr Bishop as Harry.

Diary of Miss Amelia Price

I wonder why Mr Bishop was so insistent that I show Mrs Marsden the rest of the outhouses? She liked the dairy, but I find it extraordinary that someone should not know about butter and cream, although she assured me she knew a cow when she saw one. I offered to teach her to milk, and as we began the lesson, Mr Bishop came in and told us he thought she would be very good at it, her hands having been occupied in similar fashion before.

She laughed, and he looked put out, and then the cow kicked over the bucket.

I suppose it is London manners, since both of them come from there.

Sophie

Amelia is to play for me, and she is a mess of nerves. I have never seen anyone wring their hands in real life (it happens on the stage, and in my dealings with gentlemen, fairly frequently).

'I'm not very good,' she says as though she is about to burst into tears.

'Calm yourself. Pray choose a piece you like.' I'm hoping she is indeed not too competent, for then I would have nothing to teach her. I am not so concerned about earning my keep – for sure, this is much easier than being a mistress, and I do not have to put up with snoring, among other unpleasantness, at night – but I like this young girl, her awkward charm and innocence. I want to help her.

'You see . . .' She paws miserably through the book of music. 'I don't know how to . . . that is, I've never had lessons.'

'You mean you cannot read music?'

'No, I don't know how. Aunt Shad tried to teach me, but she had to keep running out to vomit.'

'What! Your playing was so bad?'

She shakes her head, taking my jest entirely seriously. 'No, she was with child. Besides, Aunt Shad doesn't really like to play. She likes horses and babies better.'

'But you can play?'

'Oh yes. It's quite easy.' She sits at the pianoforte and hums quietly to herself. 'This is the Sussex Waltz.'

And she plays, quite sweetly and simply, a tune she must have danced to. Her touch is light and delicate, but she has an instinct for when she should play loud or soft. I am charmed and impressed.

'Where did you hear it?' I ask when she has finished.

'Oh, everyone knows this.' She looks at me with astonishment as though everyone can do what she can.

'I see. Would you like to sing for me?'

She looks much happier and we browse through the volume of music together to find a song she knows, and naturally it is from Shakespeare, Feste's song from the conclusion of *Twelfth Night*. I am struck not only by her innocence (it is, after all, a bawdy and vulgar song) but by her pure tone and the way she phrases the words.

'I know I don't know very much,' she says after I have played the last chord.

'On the contrary, you know much more than you

think. I'm afraid you'll have to learn how to read music but your touch on the instrument is very fine and you sing extremely well.'

'Oh. Thank you. Do you think I know enough to go on the stage?'

'I really couldn't say, Amelia. I don't think Lord or Lady Shad would wish me to encourage such ambitions. There is a great deal of difference between playing for polite society in a drawing room and performing on a stage with hundreds of people watching, ready to jeer if they do not like what you do, and—'

I stop abruptly. I do not want to reveal my theatrical experience, but I regret it is too late.

'Indeed?' She looks thrilled. 'What must you do on the stage?'

I close the volume of music. 'You have to make your voice reach the furthest seats in the house. You have to learn to breathe properly and— and, above all remember you are a lady.'

For, yes, as though responding to a prompter, Harry Bishop has entered the room and frowns at us both. 'Why, just in time!' I cry. 'Mr Bishop must partner you. I shall play a country dance and see how your deportment is.'

He bows to Amelia, but not to me. 'So we should pretend this is an Assembly, Miss Amelia?'

'Oh, indeed, yes!' Amelia smiles at him.

'Lady Shad asked me to send for you, but it is not a

pressing matter. Pray instruct your pupil, Mrs Marsden.'

Oh, damn the man again. I have not been to a country assembly in my life. I cannot think of one time where I have danced in polite company. On tables, yes. In taverns. On stages. But at a country assembly?

I recover quickly. 'The gentleman will ask you to dance, Miss Amelia.' A fairly logical step, I'd think, but his cynical smile tells me otherwise. 'He has of course been introduced to us by a mutual acquaintance.'

He bows, she curtsies, and I take my place at the pianoforte, having found a country dance in the music collection, very ill copied (Lady Shad's, I suspect). I watch Harry and Amelia dance, or rather they play at dancing, sometimes imagining other couples within a set, and parting to take invisible hands or smile at non-existent companions. It is quite charming and innocent. Harry, slightly uncomfortable at first, takes his part well, encouraged by her ease and happiness – I can tell she is a creature who loves to dance, but what young woman does not? They step and circle, well matched, and my fingers stumble on the keys. I recover from my spurt of wrong notes, and they catch the rhythm again, laughing now, and apparently oblivious to everything except each other.

'Enough, I think.' I conclude the dance with a crashing chord. They stop, Harry shaking his head and laughing, and she blushing a little.

'Why did you stop, Mrs Marsden?'

Why did I stop, indeed? I'm not sure. I don't altogether approve of what I have just witnessed, although as I tell myself, there has been nothing untoward. Their dance was fanciful but not improper and I cannot tell why it has disturbed me so. I look at Amelia. I do not want to look at Harry.

'You know well what you are about, Amelia.' There is a certain shrillness to my tone and she looks at me with surprise. 'That is to say, your manner is natural and easy and I think you will do well enough at any . . . any . . .'

'Are you quite well, Mrs Marsden?' Harry has come to my side.

'Very well, I assure you. This room is a little close, that is all. Come, Amelia, we must visit Lady Shad, and . . .' I cannot finish my sentences, apparently, but I take Amelia's arm and escort her into the morning room, where Lady Shad lounges on the sofa, Harriet at her breast, and her two sons play with a battered set of lead soldiers upon the floor.

'Amelia is a very talented musician,' I tell Lady Shad and see Amelia blush with pride.

'I've always thought so, but I can barely tell one tune from another. I find her singing very restful. Shad said we should ask your advice about a new gown for Amelia.' She pulls a tattered London newspaper from her side. It is some six months old. 'You know all about London fashions, do you not?'

'A little.' To my horror, the newspaper falls open at a sketch of the supremely elegant Mrs Wallace's new gown.

'I thought a nice muslin, maybe spotted, or a striped cotton. What say you, Mrs Marsden?'

I remember that gown, palest muslin with a gold net overlay, cut scandalously low with the barest hint of sleeves. Dear Charlie could hardly wait to get it off me.

'Perhaps the cut of the bosom . . .' I venture.

'Yes, I suppose so.' Lady Shad glances down at her own generous bosom, enhanced by nursing an infant. 'We cannot all be so fortunate.'

'Who is Mrs W—?' Amelia asks, peering at the sketch. 'She looks a little like you, Mrs Marsden, except you are much prettier.'

'She is a lady of a certain reputation, Amelia, and if you understand that and we were in polite society, you would pretend you did not know what I mean.'

Amelia looks rather dumbfounded at Lady Shad's advice. 'Why, Aunt Shad?'

'Mama, we need the newspaper.' Master George, his face set in a determined frown, sits on the sofa and watches his sister nurse. 'When will she be big enough to play with me?'

'Not for a good while yet,' his mother says, ruffling his hair. 'What do you need the newspaper for?'

'It's complicated,' the child says.

His mother tears the picture out of the newspaper and hands the rest to her son, who then borrows the scissors from her workbox and joins his brother on the floor again.

'Amelia, you should go into the village and visit the dressmaker,' Lady Shad says. 'Mrs Marsden can advise you on the cloth and cut, for I don't think Mrs Henney is up on the London fashions, even those from six months ago. We're invited to Captain and Mrs Carstairs next week and I daresay there'll be dancing. They're our neighbours, Mrs Marsden, and she's quite amiable although he has but one leg and is dreadfully shy. And after that we go to Brighton, for the Beresfords have invited us – he is Shad's cousin, you know, and Lady Beresford my great friend. Do you know Brighton, Mrs Marsden?'

Brighton! Oh heavens, of course I do. I cannot possibly go there, not even disguised as a frump. What on earth shall I do?

'George is cutting Simon's hair again,' Amelia says. She reaches for the scissors, which George relinquishes after a brief struggle.

Sure enough, his brother's hair is reduced to tufts, and Simon gives a delighted smile at the attention.

'You little monsters,' Lady Shad says with great affection. 'And when shall you be breeched, George, a great boy like you?'

George sticks his thumb in his mouth and frowns.

'Very well.' His mother shrugs. 'But if you wish to go into the village with the ladies you must wear breeches.'

Both little boys giggle and crowd on to the sofa with their mother and I am charmed with this demonstration of familial affection.

Lord Shad enters the drawing room, a boot in his hand. 'Which of you fiends pissed in my boot this morning?' He pounces on George. 'You? And you've cut your brother's hair again. Ma'am, I'll be grateful if you do not lend your child your scissors, and pray teach him the difference between a boot and a chamber pot.'

'Papa, I did it,' Simon says, and then, 'George told me to.'

'A conspiracy! Come with me, both of you.' He leaves with his sons, who seem quite cheerful and not at all contrite.

'Oh. He will not beat them?' Amelia looks mightily distressed.

'No, he's too soft-hearted. Doubtless he teaches them a lesson with soap and a brush in the kitchen, and I regret there is nothing they like better than soap bubbles and getting themselves wet. But at least they will be clean for a little while.' She glances at me. 'Mrs Marsden, my apologies for our irregular house. Bishop will drive you into the village; I know he has some business to conduct there.'

Diary of Miss Amelia Price

I write this with the greatest of excitement as I have come upstairs to get my spencer as we are to drive into the village where I will get a new gown (!!!), and today I danced with Mr Bishop and he is a very good dancer and I enjoyed it exceedingly. I think Mrs Marsden thought it improper but I am sure if she had she would have said. And tho he danced with me he looked at her quite a lot. And now I must go.

Harry

I am none too pleased at Lady Shad's command to drive Sophie and Amelia into the village but I am to buy some household goods, tea and sugar, and collect a sack of flour from the mill and can think of no reason why they should not accompany me. The two women spend a vast deal of time getting ready – my mother and sisters are the same – and I stand for a good ten minutes becoming increasingly impatient while the horse dozes.

They appear giggling and both looking remarkably pretty until I remind myself that Amelia is my employer's ward and Sophie – Mrs Marsden, that is – is a strumpet in the clothing of respectability. As soon as they are in the trap the horse stirs itself, cocks its tail, and deposits a heap of steaming manure on the cobbles of the stableyard. For some reason I am mortified, but not nearly as much as when, but a few minutes later, the horse and I have a struggle of wills as to whether it shall remain on the road or take a turn.

'His friend lives down there.'

'His friend, Miss Amelia? How can a horse have a friend?' I haul at the reins and click my tongue.

'His friend is a donkey. Would you like me to take the reins, Mr Bishop?'

'No thank you, ma'am.' We lurch back on to the road. It is a warm day and if I were alone I would divest myself of my coat, but of course with the two females present it is impossible.

Amelia, seated next to me, rummages in her reticule and produces a piece of newspaper, turning to speak to Sophie who sits behind. I glance idly at the newspaper and drop the whip. 'Why do you have that?'

'It's a picture of a gown,' Amelia explains. 'It's very fashionable.'

'But it's—'

'The notorious Mrs W—' Sophie murmurs and I glance back. Her face is hidden by the brim of her bonnet yet I could swear she laughs at me.

I scrabble to retrieve the whip from the floor of the cart and place it in the holder where it can do no harm, considering I shall not need it again until our return journey when doubtless the horse will again wish to pay a morning call. I have learned to ride and drive from necessity, not as a right from birth, or from being reared in the country.

This is my first visit to the village, where a venerable oak spreads its branches over a few boys playing ball on the green and a collection of ducks swimming in a small, muddy pond. I have no doubt Amelia casts a professional eye upon them. I let the two ladies down at a shop with a window full of bonnets and fabrics, whose sign proclaims it to be the establishment of one Mrs Henney, and spend some time at the grocer's in the village, where I am treated with much deference before the owner launches into a torrent of praise for the departed Mr Roberts, my predecessor.

After a brief struggle with the horse, who has decided we should return home immediately, I return to the dressmaker's. The bell clangs as I enter female territory and I am reminded of the tedium and mystery of visiting such establishments with my sisters and mother. Amelia and Sophie pore over piles of fabric and trims at the counter.

A soft stream of chatter comes from Mrs Henney. '. . . and born not six months after the wedding, and a fine lusty child he is, but he has bright red hair. Well. I am sure I need say no more. Now I did hear also that the serving maid at the vicar's has gone to visit her mother and she had grown very stout these last few weeks; of course I am not the gossiping sort, but . . .'

'Mr Bishop!' cries Amelia, having looked up at the jangle of the bell, and, blinking, recognized me. 'You must help us decide. Pale blue or cream? I am afraid if I choose the cream, my gloves will not match for I am sure they will look dingy. Or the pink, do you think?'

'Oh, the pink, most definitely.' Frankly I have no idea, but it is obvious a firm masculine sensibility is needed here.

'Pink?' She turns to Sophie. 'Oh. But I thought you said—'

'So I did. Take no notice of Mr Bishop. His response was merely to get us out of the door and himself out of this distressingly feminine atmosphere. He has not even looked at the fabrics. No, I stand by the blue. Mrs Henney, I am sure you can use some leftover fabric to fashion a bandeau for Miss Amelia . . .' and they are off again.

Mrs Henney drops me a curtsy and offers me tea while the ladies' business continues. It seems they are coming to a conclusion, although the mention of the bandeau creates some time-consuming excursions into consideration of various silk flowers, of which Mrs Henney possesses an alarming quantity.

'But what shall you wear, Mrs Marsden?' Amelia cries and I groan, probably silently, fearing the whole process will start all over again.

'Do not concern yourself, Amelia. I have a perfectly acceptable gown. Besides, I shall play the piano while the guests dance, and I do not wish to outshine the guests.'

'And very proper for a widowed lady, ma'am,' Mrs Henney comments, almost certainly a widowed lady herself. She sports a monstrosity of a cap, lace and starch with strange side flaps that make her look like a goat. 'Now then, let us see . . .' Business is concluded, for she scribbles on a piece of paper, with the ragged piece of newspaper at her elbow for inspiration.

Sophie pauses to examine a Kashmir shawl, vividly patterned.

'Oh, you should buy it!' Amelia cries.

Mrs Henney looks up from her calculations. 'Indeed, ma'am, you should. Very few ladies have the complexion to carry off such bright colours.'

Sophie drapes the shawl over one shoulder and gazes at herself in the mirror. 'It's very pretty.' She shakes her head. 'No, I think not.'

She gives a regretful glance to the shawl, placing it back on its stand, before beginning a discussion with Amelia about the bonnet in the window with as much dedication and energy as members of the Royal Society pondering a scientific specimen. Now it is my turn at the counter to arrange for payment (billed to Lord Shad) and delivery of the gown and its odds and ends.

'How much is the shawl Mrs Marsden admired?' I ask Mrs Henney.

She mentions a sum that makes me blink, adding, 'Such a pretty young woman should not hide her light under a bushel.'

'True, ma'am. Please add it to the purchases, with Mrs Marsden's name on the package.' I slide a guinea on to the counter. 'We need not encumber his lordship with the cost.'

'I see, sir,' she says, her voice heavy with meaning, and I realize that my plan already has consequences I should have considered. From what I have seen of Mrs Henney, word will spread like wildfire that Mr Bishop has intentions towards pretty little Mrs Marsden. I wave away the change. 'It shall be our secret, eh, Mrs Henney?'

The coin disappears into the lady's lace mitten. 'Certainly, sir. Certainly.'

Sophie

The next week passes pleasantly enough. I see very little of Harry, whose frowning countenance unsettles me. I know he plans some mischief and it is probably against me, but I cannot dwell upon his intentions. I spend about half of each day with Amelia, teaching her how to read music. She is somewhat put out to discover that not only are there sharps, but that she must also deal with flats too, and grumbles a little. She learns a couple of songs which were all the rage in London a year ago, printed in another newspaper yellowing with age that the children have not yet purloined.

Occasionally she wonders why his lordship is so very insistent that this invitation be treated with such great care. After all, she has been to Captain Carstairs' house a dozen times before. We speculate on the possibility that young gentlemen, new to the neighbourhood, have been invited also, or even a party from London;

or that it is practice for her social engagements in Brighton.

'Do you think I need to learn to flirt?' she asks with absolute sincerity.

'I think you will find out how to do it.'

'Maybe I should practise on Mr Bishop.'

'On Mr Bishop!' I echo. 'Oh, surely not.'

'I don't think he would mind. He is very good-natured. Just yesterday he spent all afternoon making a hutch for John's rabbits.'

'I don't think it would be proper. Flirting is hardly the female equivalent of carpentry.' The claim of impropriety is the best way to end an argument with Amelia, particularly one where I am not sure what my high moral ground should be. And Mr Bishop good-natured? I have yet to see him so, but he is always most proper on the rare occasions we meet. He dines a couple of times with the family that week, unfailingly polite, meeting Lady Shad's teasing with a fine ironic air and discussing work to be done on the house with Lord Shad.

One afternoon I look out of the window to see him, in his shirtsleeves, playing cricket with John and the two little boys. He may keep my secret, but all in all he seems far more at home in this house than I do. I find I must second-guess every thought and gesture. I sigh and watch Harry carefully miss an easy catch and go chasing after the ball while little Simon, skirts tucked up, runs between the wickets and Master George jumps up and down with excitement, crying encouragement to his brother.

It is with great excitement that Amelia and I receive the package from Mrs Henney, only a few hours before we are expected at the Carstairs' house.

From her usual place on the sofa, Harriet on her lap, Lady Shad directs the unwrapping, thriftily stowing away the brown paper in which the gown is wrapped. 'I almost wish I could come,' she murmurs. 'If only this sweet little wretch did not occupy my person all day and all night.'

Lord Shad, fingers stained with watercolours, strolls in and bends to kiss his wife. 'We'll hire a wet nurse.' He tickles his daughter's stomach. 'She's smiling.'

'Certainly not! To both of your suggestions. That is wind, you should know by now.'

'Oh!' Amelia holds up the gown and smiles at herself in the mirror above the fireplace and I'm gratified to see that the blue was the right choice for her. 'Oh, Uncle Shad, this is the most lovely gown I have ever had. Thank you, sir.'

'You do me credit, my dear.' Lord Shad sits on the sofa next to his wife and takes their daughter on to his knee.

'Wait. What's this?' Lady Shad draws a small parcel

from among the swathes of brown paper. 'Why, Mrs Marsden, something for you.'

'For me? I bought nothing.'

I take the brown paper parcel and regretfully my mind leaps to the immediate conclusion, that there is only one person who could have made such a gesture, and that is my employer. He has been perfectly proper towards me although he is obviously a man who appreciates a pretty woman; I have seen admiration in his glance from time to time, but not nearly as often as I have seen pure adoration directed towards his wife and children. But this . . . coming as I do from a world where gentlemen, married or not, give women like myself gifts for one purpose, what else can I think? He is a handsome man, and however fond he may be of his wife, she has but recently given birth, and I know all too well that gentlemen in that situation often look elsewhere for gratification.

And I thought he might be different!

My face heats.

'Oh, do unwrap it,' Amelia says.

I take a deep breath. 'Surely this is a mistake. It must be something for you, Amelia, an appreciation of your patronage of Mrs Henney's establishment.'

Amelia giggles. 'Your name is written on it.'

'Oh. So it is.'

Lady Shad watches with bright interest and I cannot

bear that she is to suffer embarrassment and disillusion.

I hate that Amelia is to witness this also and her evening will in all likelihood be ruined. 'Amelia, why don't you go to my bedchamber and ask one of the maids to help you change into the gown? We should like to see you wear it, and we may have to check the hem.'

'Thank you, Mrs Marsden.' She gives another glance at the parcel that is burning a hole in my conscience. Surely I have not encouraged his lordship? Or am I so used to playing the whore that without an awareness of what I do I have made my intentions and profession clear?

The door closes behind us. Harriet burbles quietly.

'Is something wrong, Mrs Marsden?' Lord Shad asks.

I shake my head, hoping I am mistaken.

'Mrs Marsden?' With a smile, Lady Shad offers me a pair of embroidery scissors.

Resisting the temptation to plunge the scissors into the bosom of her faithless husband, I cut the string and unwrap the parcel. Folds of scarlet and blue and cream tumble and drape on to my lap. It is the Kashmir shawl that I admired and I wonder how on earth Lord Shad knew of it. Did Harry tell him how I admired it?

I stand, folding the shawl over my arm. I cannot resist stroking the gorgeous sheen of the fabric. 'My lord, I regret I cannot accept this gift.'

I wait to be told to pack my bags and leave.

'Eh?' Lord Shad looks up from playing with his daughter's hands. 'Very pretty, Mrs Marsden, but there's nothing I can do if it displeases you. Return it, I'd suggest, although the colours look remarkably well on you. Besides, you'll need something of the sort in Brighton, won't she, my dear?'

'Oh, of course you should keep it.' Lady Shad reaches out a hand to touch the shawl. 'It's beautiful. I wish it were mine, but it would only be covered with puke or the boys would borrow it for a tent. So who bought it for you, Sophie? Surely it is not from a secret admirer?'

Lord Shad yawns. 'Harry Bishop, I expect.'

Harry Bishop? I cannot believe my employer to be so underhand as to implicate his steward! 'I assure you, my lord, I have no intentions of any sort towards Mr Bishop or any other gentleman!'

He shrugs. 'I trust you'll wear it tonight, ma'am.'

I dare not look at Lady Shad, who must surely be aware of her husband's proclivities, and wonder again at her nonchalance but she has taken the child again.

To my great relief at that moment Amelia enters the room, resplendent in her finery, and we exclaim over her beauty and that of her gown but the evening is spoiled for me.

Harry

I have regretted my folly a dozen times already this past week, although kept busy enough with the house and in particular Lord Shad's plan to make the parlour modern, knocking out part of the wall to accommodate a room for plants and thence building steps and flower-beds leading to the garden itself. He has produced several sketches and we are both eager to demolish the wall without bringing the house down around ourselves. I am sworn to secrecy for it is a gift for Lady Shad, to be accomplished while the family is at Brighton.

I spend more time than a rational man should dressing for the evening. This is the country so silk knee breeches are not required (fortunate for I own none) but I take care with the knot of my neckcloth and brush my coat. I do not intend to impress Sophie, merely to maintain my dignity if she spurns the shawl. What, indeed, was I thinking in the purchase of such an extravagant item? Extravagant for me, that is. I daresay she has owned a dozen such shawls, all finer.

All three footmen, Matthew, Mark and Luke, wish to accompany us, for naturally they have friends in the Carstairs' house, but a mile or so away, and I choose one-eyed Matthew, who boasts two arms and two legs. Mark, who has assumed his best false hand, a strange, lumpy appendage forced into a glove, looks particularly disappointed.

Lord Shad and I wait with Matthew in the hall for Sophie and Amelia. He frowns and consults his watch. 'What the devil are women that they cannot be on time?' And then he breaks into one of those smiles that I imagine has made many a woman tremble as he sees his ward and her companion descend the staircase.

Yes, Sophie wears the shawl and her beauty takes my breath away.

Sophie

I really do not care at all for the way Harry Bishop looks at Amelia as we descend the staircase. It is most improper. And I refuse to look at Lord Shad in whom I am deeply disappointed. I pity his wife.

Since the house is so close, we walk over the fields, with a footman carrying our dancing slippers in a burlap sack. We keep country hours here, so dinner is at four and it is still bright and sunny, with great clouds floating above.

'If they ask me to sing or play, sir, what shall I do?' Amelia asks her guardian.

'Accept, if you feel like it,' he says, smiling upon her with great fondness. 'You must begin sometime, and why not here, where your friends are?'

'I suppose so.' She bites her lip. 'What do you think, Mrs Marsden?'

I think she'll outshine any provincial miss there but I don't want to make her more nervous than she is already, or too overconfident. 'I think Lord Shad is correct.'

She smiles. 'And there'll be dancing, too!'

We arrive shortly at Captain Carstairs' house, and our host, a former Navy man, greets us with great warmth, kissing Amelia's cheek and shaking hands with Lord Shad. His wife is an affable, friendly woman who takes Amelia's arm and I realize that most of the guests are from the neighbourhood and have looked forward to seeing the new gown with great anticipation. Doubtless Mrs Henney has made sure all know of it. The young men present look upon Amelia with some interest.

Do they know also that Lord Shad has designs upon me?

Some of the ladies give me curious glances, assessing my dress and the way I have arranged my hair. The gown, which seemed so very modest and plain, now feels all too revealing, proclaiming that its wearer has embraced London fashions, the cut of the bosom a little too low, the hemline revealing a little too much ankle. The shawl seems a brazen declaration of my reputation, a pity indeed for it is a garment I fell in love with when first I saw it at the dressmaker's shop. I believe one can be said to fall in love with a piece of fabric, but I am sure

I am not the only woman who does, and, unlike the male sex, a woman knows where she is with such an item.

Since Amelia knows most of the company present she does not need to be under my wing for our hostess has taken over that duty. Lord Shad and Captain Carstairs are deep in conversation.

To my surprise it is Harry Bishop who steps forward and introduces me to the Reverend and Mrs Dimmock and their curate, Mr Dibble, the author of the ill-advised love poem to Amelia. Mr Dibble gazes at my bosom (I am used to this sort of attention and take no notice). The Reverend and Mrs Dimmock are full of praise for John and Amelia and by extension to Lord Shad and his family. I summon up polite affability and answer their questions. Yes, indeed, it is a very fine part of the country (flat, muddy, altogether too much water and sky) and the family most welcoming (so much so that his lordship expects to be welcomed into my bed at any time).

Amelia has attached herself to another young woman, the daughter of the Wilton family, so I am told by the Dibbles. Miss Jane Wilton is a pretty giggler with a headful of springy golden curls and I am glad to see that in her company, Amelia becomes something of a giggler and whisperer herself. I am reminded of meeting Lizzie and Claire for the first time at boarding school and how we knew all at once that we were to be best friends.

After a brief conversation with her friend, Amelia comes to my side. 'Mrs Marsden, Jane – that is, Miss Wilton – has invited me to accompany her family to Bath this summer! Do help me persuade Uncle Shad that I should go! I know it is not so fashionable as Brighton, but Miss Wilton and I are such great friends already.'

'Of course.' What else can I say? In a way I am relieved, for if I were to accompany Amelia there it is doubtful whether I should meet any acquaintances from my former life. Bath is not particularly fashionable these days now that the Prince Regent has made Brighton his own.

Amelia puts her arm in mine and takes me to meet the Wiltons. The party also includes Mrs Wilton's brother, a military gentleman who seems somewhat ill at ease in his brand-new regimentals, Captain Dean. 'Charmed, ma'am.'

He gazes at me with approval and for one horrid moment I fear he recognizes me, for at first glance he is just the sort of gentleman, raffish and dandyish, convinced all females will swoon at his feet, that I should have associated with in my previous profession. But no, he is a young man who feels his uniform obliges him to flirt with any pretty woman, a sort of patriotic duty. He bends over my hand, creaking and jingling as he does so.

'Oh, fie, Edward!' His sister smacks him with her fan.

'Take no notice, Mrs Marsden, he is an incorrigible flirt. Besides, next week his regiment leaves for Nottingham and we shall be bereft of his company. So, Mrs Marsden, is it not charming how well our young ladies get along? And to think Lord Shadderly . . . well. I must say, she is a most ladylike creature and she is a credit to him. And to you, ma'am, of course.'

'I regret I cannot take much credit for Amelia. Her talents are mostly her own.' I am full of admiration for Mrs Wilton's deflection of any interest I may have in her brother; not only have I been given notice that the gentleman is not long in the neighbourhood but he is not to be taken seriously. To annoy her, I add with a sigh, 'It is very fine to see a gentleman in regimentals among all these naval gentlemen.'

She snaps her fan shut but at that moment we are summoned in to dinner. It is a very informal affair for we straggle into the Carstairs' dining room and sit where we will. So it is I find myself next to Captain Dean and opposite Harry, who is deep in conversation with some other neighbours about making beer.

Captain Dean gives me the heavy-lidded, amused smile of a man who believes he is God's gift to women. 'You are very interesting, Mrs Marsden. A hothouse flower set down in the country.'

'La, sir!' I affect a giggle and smack him, a little more than playfully, across the knuckles with a spoon. 'I'll take some of that pie by your elbow, if you please.'

Breathing heavily, he helps me to a slice of pie, managing to drip gravy suggestively on to the tablecloth. (No, I cannot adequately describe how he does it. Suffice it to say that the pie becomes an object of carnal interest and I its unwitting votary.)

'And do you enjoy military life, sir?' I ask, briskly dumping a spoonful of carrots on to his plate. 'Some carrots, Mr Bishop?' For that gentleman looks upon me across the table with disapproval.

Captain Dean stirs inside his high military collar and reddens. 'I've not yet joined the regiment, ma'am.'

'Oh, so you are a chrysalis of a soldier.'

Harry Bishop drops a large slice of roast beef on to my plate while the military gentleman ponders my statement. I think he is somewhat disturbed by my implication that he is to become a martial butterfly.

'Do you enjoy walking, Mrs Marsden?'

Naturally Amelia and I spend a great deal of time splashing through puddles while she recites Shakespeare to the clouds and I try to save the hems of my gowns from mud, but I know where the Captain's question is leading. Doubtless he imagines thickets, grassy banks, secluded spots, and my own charms laid open to his attack. My reply is hesitant. Genteel ladies enjoy walking. I am a genteel lady, so therefore . . . 'Oh, very much so. But—'

'Lord Shad wishes the ladies in his household to stay indoors until the Great Norfolk Horned Beast has been captured,' Harry says.

'The Great Norfolk Horned Beast!' The Captain looks at him with astonishment as do I, for I am amazed that Harry has come to my rescue. 'What sort of creature is this?'

'Huge,' I offer. 'Possessed of great teeth and claws and the size of an elephant. And horns, hence its name.'

'Mrs Marsden exaggerates. It's the size of a small cow,' Harry says. 'It's played havoc with our sheep this past month.'

Others at the table have overheard our conversation and have taken it up, some speculating it is a creature from the Americas that has escaped from a private collection or an ancient beast haunting the fens since the dawn of time. I watch, entranced, as the topic weaves and grows in richness and inventiveness, until it reaches Lord Shad, who laughs and declares it a great piece of nonsense.

And so dinner continues, with the amorous Captain at my elbow and Harry watchful opposite me and it is mightily uncomfortable. I am indeed glad when our hostess rises, prompting a general clatter of chairs as we all get to our feet, and shawls are disentangled, fans collected, and the gentlemen bow us out of the room. I am probably the only lady there who has some idea of what will follow, the male rituals of port and tobacco and manly jests and conversation, the sideboard door open to reveal the chamberpot.

After we leave, our hostess discreetly lets it be known that a water closet is available for the ladies' use, an item she seems to be rather proud of, blushingly confessing it is a new improvement to the house. Mrs Wilton laments that such an item may increase laziness among the staff, but Mrs Carstairs assures her that the usual arrangements continue in the bedchamber. Satisfied that the social order is maintained, we progress to the drawing room where we arrange ourselves prettily on the sofas and chairs, and giggling Miss Wilton fusses with Amelia's hair. I admire the pianoforte, acquired about the same time as the water closet, Mrs Carstairs confesses.

'Did you attend many concerts in London, Mrs Marsden?' Mrs Wilton asks, an opening gambit in the game of discovering more about me, following her brother's interest in me during dinner.

'As many as I could, ma'am,' I reply with a fine ambiguity.

'Oh, London,' Mrs Carstairs says with a sigh. 'I've never been further than Norwich. I do so envy you, Mrs Marsden. But tell me, how do Charlotte and the child? I long to see her. We are godparents, you know, to little Harriet and the boys.'

I know that in the normal course of things any

fashionable lady would be expected to stay abed for at least another week, not lounge half-dressed on the sofa with her children, a contented, milky slattern, or repair to the kitchen to assist in the preparation of strawberry jam. I assure Mrs Carstairs that all is well.

'I believe that is a gown from a London dressmaker, Mrs Marsden,' Mrs Wilton interjects. 'Most elegant. With whom were you in service before?'

She has noticed my gown is far better than any a woman in my position should be able to afford and my mind becomes absolutely blank. Of course I have prepared a false story of my life, but her effrontery in asking me about my previous employment, as though she was considering me for a position as chambermaid, fairly takes my breath and my fabricated story away. Mrs Carstairs glances from her to me with some distress, clutching an album of music to her bosom.

I am saved from a reply by the entry of the gentlemen led by Captain Carstairs, deep in conversation with Lord Shad, and Mrs Wilton's attention, and that of the rest of the ladies, turns to the gentlemen. There is a fair amount of laughter and banter and a great gust of brandy accompanies them into the room. Mrs Carstairs, who has interposed herself between me and Mrs Wilton, shares a relieved smile with me, and takes over pouring tea which one of her footmen hands around.

Amelia glances at the pianoforte. I thought she'd be

nervous. On the contrary, I see she longs to perform and the thought crosses my mind that maybe she might be suited for the stage. She has talent, she has ambition, and she has what I never did, a yearning that is half passion, half steely determination. I relied on my good looks, my family's influence, and a moderate talent to use the stage as a stepping stone to becoming a courtesan. I also possessed the fearlessness of youth, the one thing I have in common with Amelia (except that at her age I was already mistress to the elderly yet lecherous Lord Radding, of whom I still think with affection as I lie in the bed he bequeathed me).

Amelia fidgets like a thoroughbred at the starting gate until our hostess takes pity on her and asks if she would like to play. For the first time she hesitates and I offer to accompany her while she sings. I am afraid that my insistence that she learns to read music may have set her back a little in her playing. We confer and she chooses an opera aria we have studied that week.

She steps forward, and something twists inside me at her beauty and innocence. I shall protect her and guide her; I would say she is like a sister except my sisters needed little protection or guidance as they forged indifferent careers on the stage, somewhat more success-ful careers in gentlemen's beds, and the final achieve-ment of matrimony and respectability (all except for poor Kate, dead in childbirth).

Of our audience, some of the gentlemen, who have succumbed to sleep in anticipation of musical entertainment, sit bolt upright, blinking in astonishment at what they hear. Of the ladies, their expressions vary between pure envy and admiration. Lord Shad listens with a proud smile.

I wish I could like him better for it.

But I concentrate on my playing, allowing Amelia to shine as she should, and when I raise my fingers from the keys there is as much of a thunder of applause as can be raised from the company. She turns to smile at me, and there is a question in her eyes – should she sing another? I shake my head, no: Leave them wanting more, a maxim that has served me well, both on and off stage.

She curtsies prettily and I remain at the piano in case any other young lady should like to sing. Amelia's new-found friend the giggler slops her way through a Scottish folk song to polite applause, and then the real business of the evening begins – the dancing.

The military butterfly alights at the end of the instrument. 'Are you to remain at that damned, beg your pardon, ma'am, that instrument all evening, Mrs Marsden? I had rather hoped you might do me the honour, ma'am.'

I express with great insincerity my regret that I am here to provide the music and assure the gentleman that I do not need anyone to turn pages for me. His sister regards him with disapproval and takes him under her wing so he may tread upon the feet and leave damp handprints upon the gowns of more deserving women.

Sophie

'Mrs Marsden, you must be tired of playing the piano while everyone dances. You have been here a good hour at least. I insist, my dear, I shall play this last one so you may dance.'

'You're most kind, Mrs Carstairs, but I assure you there is no need . . .' But my hostess waves me away and takes my place on the bench. Across the room, the amorous Captain sets his sights and begins a march towards me as though I were a besieged fort ready for the final attack. Even worse, Lord Shad rises from the sofa where he sits with Amelia, and begins his own advance. I look around and see assistance is at hand.

'Harry! I need you!'

'I beg your pardon, Mrs Marsden?'

I grab his arm and smile upon him although my teeth are gritted. 'Dance with me.'

He raises his eyebrows.

'If you please, sir,' I say, my dignity thrown to the winds. Both of my would-be suitors are closing in for the kill.

'Mrs Marsden, may I beg the honour of this dance.' He looks the advancing Captain in the eye and bows to me. Fortunately he cannot see, over his shoulder, that he has bested his employer also.

'I should be delighted, sir,' I reply. I have seen him dance, of course, that time with Amelia, and tonight, where to my surprise he was in great demand as a partner, for he moves gracefully and I am convinced has trod on few feet.

I am aware also that the only time Harry has partnered me in any sense – other than the uneasy truce we maintain – was in far more intimate circumstances. And there, it is true, he performed with some clumsiness, but an endearing sense of amazement and eagerness to please; and, oh yes, a certain mastery and confidence as the long hours of that night wore on, which pleased me greatly. And it's Harry as he was then that I'm reminded of as we dance, as he guides and turns me, and I give myself to him with a perfect trust. The dance becomes a stylized flirtation, every touch of hand and glance containing a perfect amorous significance, and the other dancers fade into insignificance as we weave a pattern of desire.

So when the music ends, and after we have bowed

and curtsied to each other, we stand for a moment looking at each other and I see a sense of wonder on his face. Do I look the same? For the first time since that night, or possibly for the first time ever, we smile at each other.

And then it is as though we both awake and come to ourselves, laughing a little as we see we are the last couple on the floor, the other having retreated to the sides of the room. The evening is quite definitely breaking up now, with the guests moving in the general direction of their host and hostess to bid them farewell. It is time to go home.

'Mrs Marsden?'

'My lord?' I spin around at the tap on my shoulder.

'Forgive me for intruding, but I wished to let you and Bishop know that Amelia and I have been offered a lift home in the Wiltons' carriage, and as she's somewhat fatigued, I thought it best to accept it. Will you join us?'

'No thank you, sir. I prefer to walk.' I certainly don't want to risk being interrogated by Mrs Wilton or have his lordship press his leg against mine in a crowded carriage.

'If you're certain, then, for there is plenty of room. Bishop will see you safely home.'

It does cross my mind then that possibly he had approached me, not to ask me to dance, but only to offer me a lift home. Even so, he does not seem angry that I kept him waiting, and Amelia is busy chatting with her new friend; they hang upon each other as though they have known each other for years.

So Bishop and I find ourselves outside, beneath the light of a moon that is almost full, its light competing with the magical green light of ranks of glow-worms in the fields, and with the scent of honeysuckle strong upon the air.

He tells me he has given the footman leave to visit his friends in the kitchen of the house, so we are alone. He compliments me on my music.

I compliment him on his dancing.

He clears his throat.

'Did you enjoy Amelia's singing?'

'Very much. Lord Shad was pleased, too.'

'I shall probably not stay long in this position.'

'Indeed? Why is that?'

'I think Amelia will spend the rest of the summer with the Wilton family, and it would not be appropriate for me to accompany her.' Not after the way Mrs Wilton snubbed me. And I certainly cannot go to Brighton.

'And the Captain . . . ?'

'Oh, he's a fool. I think Mrs Wilton was concerned that he had any serious interest in me, which I am sure he hasn't, and I certainly don't in him. My thanks again to you for coming to my rescue. I am afraid my skirts would have been ruined by his spurs. He seeks to amuse himself while he is in the neighbourhood, but it will not be at my expense.'

'I am glad to hear you say it,' he says and turns to me, clasping my hand.

At that moment, a bird, which even I recognize (from its frequent depictions in opera) as a nightingale, bursts into song nearby. The moon is so bright it casts our shadows on to the ground.

'I regret I have not been fair to you, Sophie. I made some rash judgements concerning your character, yet from what I have observed of you ... and, damn it, Sophie, ever since you and I—'

He stops talking for the very good reason that he kisses me.

Is it only the influence of the dancing, the excellent punch served by our hosts, the moonlight, and the nightingale? I think not. It is something far more profound, a true connection, and although I know I should pull away and stop this, I will not, cannot. Just a little more, a little more, of his taste and scent and delicious strength. For at that moment I feel most romantically inclined towards Harry Bishop, who from the expression in his eyes – handsome eyes behind those spectacles, I notice as if for the first time – has succumbed also to similar madness.

But after a few delightful seconds or weeks or some immeasurable segment of time, I come to my senses. I detach myself from his person although I am extremely reluctant to do so; whatever else I had to teach him, Harry knew how to kiss and still does. 'I beg your pardon. This is unseemly.'

To my relief he does not mock me, but merely steps away with a slight inclination of his head. The only expression of any agitation is that he removes the spectacles and gives them a thorough polishing. 'Of course. You are quite right and I should beg your pardon.'

'I don't know why. There is no need. Shall we agree to forget this regrettable incident?'

'I'm not sure I can, or even that I want to.'

'A very pretty speech, sir.'

'On the contrary, Sophie, it is not mere prettiness. It is the truth.'

Although we are quite capable of apologising to – or bickering with each other, for I'm not sure which it is – until the sun rises the next morning, we set off on our way home, he taking my arm to guide me over the worst of the ruts in a most gentlemanly way.

He escorts me to the house, where one of the footmen, yawning, opens the front door and looks upon us both with interest. I am sure our polite farewell disappoints the footman, and I admit, as I trudge upstairs to my bed, I feel a certain disappointment myself. But I am a reformed character, the polite and respectable Mrs Marsden, and the only obstacle I have in my career is my employer.

I lie awake in my bed looking at the cavorting immortals above – to be sure, I have not yet become accustomed to viewing them so alone – and think about kissing Harry Bishop, and what a mistake it was, compounding my first, earlier mistake, and how nothing of the sort must ever happen again. I must certainly avoid Harry, moonlight, and nightingales in the future, or at least all three together.

As an afterthought, I rise from my bed and jam a chair beneath the door handle in case Lord Shad comes a-wandering, a gentleman clearly not in need of moonlight or nightingales.

Diary of Miss Amelia Price

Such an evening! Dear Jane admired my hair and gown and she is all that is delightful and although I have a hole in my new stocking and a slight blister from dancing I do not care. And they liked my singing. My first public performance!

But Jane whispered a very foolish thing to me, that she thinks Mrs Marsden and Mr Bishop are lovers! How absurd! They do not even like each other. They did look well dancing together, though.

Sophie

I am inclined next morning to give notice, something I hate to do, but what choice do I have? I cannot escape to Bath with Amelia and the dreadful Mrs Wilton, nor to Brighton where the ton gather, and there is also the matter of my amorous employer, in whom I am deeply disappointed. Naturally I avoid the decision, but then Amelia and I are summoned into his lordship's study, a rather plain, masculine room enlivened by nautical clutter and some pencil studies, presumably by his lordship, of his children.

'So,' Lord Shad begins, 'this matter of you going to Bath, Amelia. You wish to go with your new friend rather than to Brighton with the rest of us? For Mr and Mrs Price and Mrs Marsden will come with us to the sea. Mrs Wilton made it very clear that she will chaperone both you and Miss Jane, so Mrs Marsden's presence is not required in Bath.'

'Indeed yes, sir. I shall be sorry to be parted from everyone, but I do so like Miss Wilton. That is, sir, if it is agreeable to you.'

'Very well.' He rises and paces, hands beneath his coat-tails. In any other man I should have interpreted this as nervousness. 'You'll have some pin money, of course. Lady Shad says you should probably buy gowns and so on there. But . . .'

If Amelia were a little younger I believe she would jump up and down for joy, but she merely clasps her hands tight in her lap and beams with delight.

'You're very young,' Lord Shad continues. 'I don't expect you to return engaged or with half a dozen beaux, merely to have some pleasure there. However . . .' He pauses again and I see now he is indeed nervous. 'Although you are young, I think it is time for you to learn of your parentage. No, Mrs Marsden, you may stay—' for I have made a movement, half rising, not wishing to intrude upon a family conversation.

'If you are sure, sir,' I say.

'I am indeed. Amelia, what do you remember of your mother?'

She shakes her head. 'You do not mean Mrs Price, I think. My mother . . . I remember her voice a little. She gave me a toy, a little wooden lamb, when she left, and told me to stroke its fleece and think of her. I wore the fleece out and then the woman I served threw it on the fire. And then, sir, you found me.' She looks at him with sweet trust and love and I have the feeling that Amelia is about to suffer a great loss.

'And you have never heard more of her, or of who your father is?'

'No, sir. Oh, sir, has she come back?'

'No, I regret not. I fear she may be dead.'

'I think so, too.' She says it with great composure.

'But I have not needed her. I have Mr and Mrs Price and you, sir. And Aunt Shad, too. I am fortunate indeed.'

'The thing is this, Amelia.' Lord Shad stops in front of her. 'You and I, we share the same father. I am your half-brother.'

Her hands, clasped together in joy, now tighten so her knuckles turn white. I, sitting next to her, place my hand over hers. 'You mean I'm the wicked old lord's get?'

'Indeed, yes. As am I.'

'But— but I thought—' I can feel her tremble. 'I thought you were my father.'

'Amelia, my love.' He pulls a chair close and sits next to her. 'I went to sea when I was a boy. I didn't set foot in England again for years, not until my brother – our brother – died and I inherited the title. And that's when I found you, a little child beaten and abused as a parish servant, and knew I must take you in.'

'Out of duty?' Her voice shakes now.

'Duty and love. I'd like you to take the family name, Amelia, so I may acknowledge you properly.'

She shakes my hand away and jumps to her feet. 'So all may know me as your father's bastard!'

'No, so all may know you as my sister and an honoured member of the family. I intend to settle some money on you; not a large dowry, for I don't want you to be the prey of fortune hunters, and I certainly don't want you to consider marriage for a few years yet. You—'

'No!' She backs away from him. I go to her side and take her hand but she pushes me away. 'My true mother and father are Mr and Mrs Price. It has pleased you, my lord, to keep me as a— a plaything. You should have told me before!'

'You are right. I probably should have done.'

'Is John truly my brother?'

'By upbringing, yes. He is my nephew. Yours too. He is the son of my late brother.'

'I hate you,' Amelia says. Lord Shad flinches. 'I want to go away. I want to go to Bath and I have my own money, sir. I don't need yours and I don't need your name either.'

She turns and flees, the door to the study banging behind her, and I'm left alone with Lord Shad.

He drops into a chair and puts his face into his hands, his elbows on his desk. 'Oh dear God,' he says. 'What did I do wrong, Mrs Marsden?'

'I can hardly say, my lord.'

I don't quite know how one is supposed to break that sort of news. Amelia's world has been shattered, for I believe she thought all this time Lord Shad was her father; indeed, I did so, for the resemblance between them is so strong.

I hesitate for one moment. I do not want to desert Amelia but I certainly cannot go to Brighton. 'Sir, I wish to give you notice.'

'What!' He leans back in his chair now. 'Why? Why do you wish to leave us?'

'I think you know, my lord.'

'What?' He gazes at me with astonishment, and at that moment a footman comes into the study, bearing a handful of letters for his lordship, and I make my escape.

I go upstairs and tap on the door of Amelia's bed-chamber. I can hear the sound of weeping but she will not let me in. Back downstairs, Lady Shad is fast asleep with Harriet on the sofa. I find Master Simon and Master George in the kitchen where the entire staff seems to know what has transpired, and activities revolve around supplying Miss Amelia with treats – pastries, a posset, a glass of wine, sweetmeats.

John is there, too, eating bread and jam at the kitchen table. 'Well, *I* knew that,' he says with all the lordly superiority of a brother. 'She is a silly girl. Of course Uncle Shad isn't her father.' From the smugness in his voice I can tell he believes he is Lord Shad's natural son, and my heart sinks at the thought of yet another child about to suffer disillusion. However, that is Lord Shad's affair, not mine.

The house is in an uproar with rooms being closed and the family's possessions packed for the departure to Brighton. I take the three boys outside and let them play with sticks and stones and splash in puddles. We are joined by a couple of dogs that submit with good humour to tail-pulling and other indignities, and obligingly chase after thrown sticks. I am filled with melancholy for Amelia and for having to leave this house and family. There is nothing for it; I must return to London and find my errant father. I shall throw myself upon his generosity and tread the boards once again, a prospect that does not fill me with much pleasure.

Once the little boys are thoroughly dirty and tired enough I take them back inside the house, where the kitchen staff clean their hands and faces beneath the kitchen pump, and ply us all with food. Soon after the two smaller boys become listless and yawn, and I take them upstairs to the parlour where it is warm and cosy, and they curl up with the dogs in front of the fire. Of Lady Shad and her daughter there is no sign.

John wanders in with a book and sprawls on the sofa where he too falls asleep.

To my relief, when I tap on Amelia's bedchamber door next, she allows me to enter. She is hard at work sorting and packing clothes for the trip to Bath with a rather forced imitation of being in good spirits, chatting brightly about assemblies and concerts and whether her gowns will reveal her to be a country mouse indeed.

'I wish you could come with us,' she says. 'I suppose you will go to Brighton.'

'No. I am afraid, Amelia, I will be leaving this house.'

'But why?' She sits on her bed, a pair of half-rolled

stockings in her hand. Her lip trembles. 'I–I thought you would be here when I return.'

'I was hired as your companion and to teach you what little I could of music. I think my work here is done, although I am most sorry to leave you.'

'Where will you go?'

'I shall find another position.' At least I hope I shall.

'But— but we like you. We want you to stay. I want you to be here when I come back.' She bursts into tears.

'I am so sorry, Amelia.' I put my arm around her shoulders.

She dashes tears from her eyes. 'I won't go to Bath. Will you stay then? We shall all go to Brighton, although it is so very fashionable and I shall not see Jane.'

'No, I cannot.' I am close to tears myself now. 'Amelia, you must go to Bath with your new friend, although I beg of you, do not make Mrs Wilton any sort of example of how a lady behaves, for she is an exceedingly rude woman. Think of how you and Jane will enjoy yourselves there! You must go and then when you come back, you and Lord Shad will be the best of friends again, having had time to reflect and forgive. I know it was a shock to you to learn of your parentage.'

She shrugs. 'Well, if he is not my father I suppose having him as a brother is just as good. But I wish I had known before.' She finishes rolling the stocking and places it in her trunk, along with a leather-bound book.

'What are you reading?'

'It is nothing. It is my diary.' She lays a hand protectively upon it. 'I am sure they would let you go with them to Brighton. You could look after the boys.'

'No, I'm no nursemaid. Apparently I let them get too dirty today.'

She makes herself busy folding a petticoat. 'We shall all miss you. Mr Bishop will, I know.'

'I doubt it.' I rise. 'I must do my own packing.'

I go back downstairs and find Harry Bishop and his footmen throwing holland clothes over the furniture in the dining room.

I stop in the doorway and look at him. His coat is unbuttoned. He carries a sheaf of papers in one hand and a pencil in the other and he has a smudge of dirt on one cheekbone. His hair is ruffled and I have the urge to smooth it into tidiness.

I step forward.

Harry

'Sir, I must speak to you about my bed.'

Oh dear God, not again. 'What exactly is the problem, Mrs Marsden?'

'I have given notice, sir.'

'What!' Sophie is leaving? I tell the footmen to continue and walk over to her, drawing her outside the room so we may speak in privacy. 'But— but why?'

'I think you know.'

'No, I don't. I thought you were happy here. Is it something I did? Is it—' I feel my face heat. 'I beg of you, tell me if there are consequences of our— that is—'

'No, you fool, I'm not with child. I can take better care of myself than that, as I believe I once told you.'

'I'm sorry to see you go. What will you do?' My head is reeling. Despite my fondness for the family I cannot imagine this house without Sophie.

'I shall find my father and go back on the stage.

Apparently I'm not as good at respectability as I hoped.' She smiles, ironic and sweet, and I want to kiss her. 'But the bed. Will you store it for me here for a little while, Harry? Until I have a place for it?'

'Of course. But why do you leave? May I assist you in any way?'

She shakes her head. 'You're a good man, Harry Bishop.'

'His lordship wants to see you, Mr Bishop.' Another of the footmen emerges from the depths of the house.

As I hesitate, she holds out her hand to me. 'We should say our farewells now, Harry, for I doubt we'll get the chance to speak to each other alone again. I leave for London tomorrow.'

'But—' I take her hand in mine. 'Is it that Captain?'

'Who?'

'The Captain last night. Did— does he—'

'No, no.' She laughs. 'I think his sister frightened him off any entanglement with me. No, it is – but never mind. You'd best go and see his lordship. He, better than anyone in this house, knows why I must leave. Wait.' She licks a finger and rubs my cheek. 'That's better. Goodbye, Harry.'

Her other hand falls from mine and she walks away, going up the stairs with none of her usual grace and liveliness, her head bowed.

Lord Shad! She speaks of him? Surely she is

mistaken. I have been in service nearly all my life, since I left home at the age of ten. I know why women, particularly pretty ones, leave positions in households; it happens all too often.

I find Lord Shad in his study where he is surrounded by heaps of paper, although at the moment he is busy packing his painting things.

'What the devil have I done, Bishop? I'm surrounded by a house full of wailing women, none of whom will speak to me, not that Harriet can, although she screams half the night instead. So.' He points to the papers. 'These papers relate to the improvements on the house. Bulmersh the builder will be here with his men tomorrow. Pray make sure he knocks the wall out in the drawing room and no other. What the devil did you do to Mrs Marsden?'

'I beg your pardon, sir?'

'Did you debauch her?'

'My lord! I most certainly did not. It was another whose advances she feared and against whom she had no protection.'

I wait, expecting his lordship to sack me, but instead he places a handful of paintbrushes on to his desk. 'Sit.' His voice is icy cold.

I do so and he drops into the chair opposite and regards me for a long, uncomfortable moment, which gives me time enough to imagine my return to London and to the hotel and my parents' disappointment and bewilderment. 'From what you say, I can only deduce,' he says after I have imagined the worst, 'that Mrs Marsden believed that very handsome shawl to be a gift from me. Why is that so, Harry? No, I'll tell you why. Because you had neither the courage nor sense to declare yourself to her.'

I clench my fists, longing, for the first time in my life, to punch someone. 'I— I thought she knew.'

He shrugs. 'Apparently not, although everyone else did. But who am I to judge you so? Everyone else except poor little Amelia knew of her true parentage and now I have yet another unhappy female casting me black glances. So what shall you do, Harry?'

'I don't know, my lord. She is determined to leave tomorrow.'

He bangs his clenched fist on the surface of his desk. 'Declare yourself. Have the banns called. You do intend marriage, I trust?'

'Of course, my lord.' I suppose I do. I hadn't really thought much beyond seeing her wear the shawl. 'I bought her the shawl on a whim, because she liked it, and because I thought she should have something pretty, my lord. I—'

'You're in love.'

'I—'

'Go, Bishop, and repair the damage. Tell her she may

join us at Brighton if she wishes to stay in our employ. And this is a wedding gift unless she refuses . . .' He produces a soft leather bag and places it in my hand. 'Pray give it to Mrs Marsden, for I shall not see her go penniless if you blunder further. She may turn you down for not speaking before. I am not a rich man but I am an honourable one. She may think what she wants of me, but you are the one who must prove himself.'

'Thank you, my lord.'

He comes around the desk and claps me on the shoulder. 'I expect this to be all settled upon my return, and the house still standing.'

Sophie

'What shall we do without you?' Lady Shad is in tears. She has retired to her bed with her three children and a battered copy of *Gulliver's Travels* from which she was reading aloud when I knocked at the bedchamber door.

'Forgive me,' I mumble, overcome with guilt.

Another knock at the door and John slouches in, followed by the dogs. 'I don't want you to go, either,' he says, and flings himself on to the bed. The dogs follow, one of them stretching its head to give the infant Harriet's face a thorough licking. Lady Shad swats the dog away.

'I came here for some peace,' she says, looking with dismay at her bed full of children and dogs. She blows her nose. 'The thing is, my dear Sophie, I am not the sort of woman who indulges in fantasies of ill health but I find myself quite out of sorts after Harriet's birth. I hope the sea air will do me good. I had hoped to have you with us at Brighton. If you are determined to leave us, you must write to us, my dear, and tell us where you are, and we shall send you word how Amelia does in Bath.'

'I am afraid it is impossible for me to stay, ma'am.'

'I am sorry for it. I believe I know the source of your discomfort.'

I am shocked that she speaks so calmly of her husband's infidelity. 'Ma'am, I assure you I gave him no encouragement whatsoever.'

'Naturally it would not be an easy situation for you. I wish you had spoken to me of it before.'

'How could I?'

'Quite easily, I should think. I am very fond of Harry, but he should have behaved with more propriety. Shad or I could have set him straight had you asked.'

'Harry!' I echo.

'He has very good taste. That shawl must have set him back a pretty penny and it suits your complexion exceedingly well.'

Oh, what a fool I have been. Harry!

'Are you engaged yet?' Lady Shad continues with a kindly if inexorable air.

'No. No. He has not asked me.'

'I'll have a word with him.'

'Ma'am, I beg of you, do not.'

'Mama, read now.' George tugs at his mother's sleeve.

'Manners, George,' I say, sounding for all the world like a governess.

'If you please, Mama,' he says with great docility. 'Mama, Mrs Marsden let us get dirty. I like her. Tell her she is not to go.'

She hands the book to me. 'If you will, Mrs Marsden. You have such a pretty voice.' She pushed the dogs aside and places Harriet on her lap to make room for me on the bed.

We dine in the bedchamber, as it is one of the few rooms not affected by the servants' preparations for the family's departure. John leaves to join Shad and Harry, who are to dine in milord's study. Amelia eats her dinner with Mr and Mrs Price and their other daughter.

After dinner, buckets of hot water are brought upstairs and Lady Shad subjects her small sons to a vigorous scrubbing and lets them run around the room completely undressed, after which, dressed in clean nightshirts and looking like small angels, they climb back into the bed.

Harriet wakes and babbles quietly to herself, clad in

a clean napkin and full of good humour, and submits herself to tickling from her brothers. 'It will not last,' Lady Shad says. 'At one in the morning she will scream until dawn. You are lucky you do not hear it at your end of the house. Let us send for another bottle of claret.'

What with the claret, a further chapter or two of *Gulliver's Travels*, and the example of the children falling asleep beside us, Lady Shad and I are rudely awakened by the entrance of her husband.

'Good God!' He places a candlestick on a tallboy and regards the occupants of the marital bed. 'Everyone, leave!'

'Even me, my dear?' Lady Shad murmurs.

'I suppose you and the children may stay. Mrs Marsden, charming though it is to find you in my bed, I must ask you and the dogs to depart. Beg your pardon, ma'am, that was most unmannerly.' His lordship carries a faint whiff of brandy about his person. As he speaks he removes his coat and waistcoat.

Alarmed that my employer is about to undress before me, I search for my shoes, abandoned somewhere on the floor near the bed. Lord Shad says, 'I have set Bishop straight, Mrs Marsden. I trust you'll reconsider your resignation and now I wish you joy and goodnight to you.'

The dogs yawn and stretch and decide they will accompany me to my own bedchamber, where they settle upon the covers leaving me a meagre space at the edge of the bed. They may be large and uncomfortable bedfellows (they have frequent dreams of the chase, paws scrabbling at the covers) but they are of some comfort, for that night I do not dream of murdering Jake Sloven.

The next morning Harry Bishop and I stand on the front steps of the house, waving as the family's carriage drives away. I quite envy them going to the sea, for I must return to London and its summer stink. My bag is packed and I intend to walk to the crossroads in the village to catch the stage.

'Mrs Marsden?'

Harry stands before me, polishing his spectacles, thus impeding my entry back into the house.

'Yes, Mr Bishop?'

To my astonishment he drops on to one knee before me and replaces the spectacles on his nose. 'Madam, I offer you my hand in marriage.'

'What? Oh, do get up, Harry, you look ridiculous.'

'I believe it is the customary position.' But he gets to his feet.

'You don't really want to marry me, do you?'

'Of course I do. Lord Shad said I should and I assure you—'

'Lord Shad has nothing to do with this. Why did you

not say something to me? Why did you let me think Lord Shad had given the shawl to me and had designs upon my person?'

He scratches his head. 'I thought you knew it was from me. Who else could have given it to you? And I am surprised you would think Lord Shad so dishonourable.'

'He is a man. I have low expectations of your sex.'

'Lord Shad advised me to marry you, ma'am. After all, with your scandalous past a respectable match is unlikely.'

'How dare you!' I slap his face and he steps back, looking shocked and hurt, and I see my refusal of his offer has injured more than his vanity.

'I beg your pardon.' He reaches inside his coat and brings out a bag. 'At least, I beg of you to accept—'

I dash the bag from his hand and guineas clink and roll down the steps, sparkling in the sunlight. 'Could you be any more insulting, sir?'

'It is from his lordship. It is customary to give a departing servant a gift.'

'Indeed.'

A cough nearby makes us both turn to see a cartload of men, holding carpentry tools. They are watching us with avid interest on their faces and I wonder how long they have been there. 'Mr Bishop, good morning, sir,' cries their leader. 'Beg pardon for the interruption, sir, but where do you want us to start work?'

'Ma'am.' Harry bows to me and goes down the steps to direct the workmen to the side of the house. The last glimpse I have of Harry – and I hope it will be the last indeed – is of him picking up guineas from the steps of the house as I walk back inside.

I feel like weeping and I do not want him to see the tears in my eyes. To be sure, our meeting was unfortunate, although I had felt that more recently we had a certain understanding with each other; certainly we could tolerate each other's company. Not to mention that startling and wonderful kiss. At any time he could have gone to Lord Shad and told him who I really was, for despite my threats, I would have had little credibility thereafter.

Worse, I had thought he liked me. That he should consider marriage with me to advance his career, as it almost certainly would, and out of pity for me – he has injured me deeply.

My bag stands in the hall, a pathetic collection of my worldly goods. I walk up the stairs and tap on the door of Amelia's bedchamber, but when I push open the door, the room is empty, the bed stripped. So she has left already. There is nothing more to keep me in this house.

My foot bumps against something in the shadowed area beneath the bed and I bend to pick it up. It is a familiar, leather-covered notebook which I recognize as

Amelia's diary, lying facedown and discarded in the dust. I brush off the cover and turn it over.

Distress has made her normally neat handwriting ragged and her sentences erratic.

I am so unhappy I think I shall die. But I do not know why. It is as Lord Shad says, I am still of the family and he too is a son of the monstrous old lord, but all my life I have heard stories of how the man I now know is my father whipped dogs and bullied people on the estate and his wife died of a broken heart. They say he was in league with the devil. Yet when I first met Lord Shad and he took me from that place where the woman beat me and asked if I would live with Mr and Mrs Price I thought he was my papa. I was only six and people were either children like me or grown-up men and women. I should not mind being Lord Shad's bastard. Why did he not tell me before?

It is all lies. Lies I have told myself but no one thought to tell me the truth.

To think that last night I was dreaming of new gowns and Bath and Jane my new friend and now it is all in ruins.

I am the wicked old lord's bastard and I cannot bear to be with anyone who knows me, even if they love me.

I am determined to go to London and become

an actress. Mrs Marsden has told me my voice is equal to that of many who perform professionally and I have long since dreamed of becoming an actress. This is my chance. All that remains is to go early to the Wiltons as planned but tell them I leave with the family for Brighton – I shall make some excuse – and then board the stage for London.

I shall work hard. I shall be good. Mrs Marsden will be proud of me.

I am so horrified I believe I will faint. I drop into a chair, the diary clutched in my hands, and read it again. Amelia believes she will walk into London unscathed and pursue a career as an actress, and although she stands as good a chance as any, I fear she will pay the price with her innocence and virtue.

And it is my fault. I had thought I had been discreet about my past as an actress. I had not wanted to encourage her, but apparently I did.

I stand and, the diary in my hands, run down the stairs.

Harry

'Harry!'

I turn, and all the workmen stop too, amid a litter of rubble and dust. I had not expected to see her so soon, if ever at all.

'Good God, what are you doing?'

'We're building a conservatory for Lady Shad. It is a surprise for her.'

She sniffs and looks around at the carnage that was once the drawing room. 'It most certainly will be. Harry, I must speak with you.'

I brush most of the dust off myself and don my coat again. The demolition has been as enjoyable as I anticipated, but it has made a filthy mess, and I leave a trail of dusty footprints across the floorboards.

I see now she is highly agitated. She clutches her pelisse and bonnet in one hand and a book of some sort in the other.

'I must go to London immediately!'

'Of course. I'll get one of the footmen to—'

'Give me that money, if you please.'

'You mean the money Lord Shad wanted to give you?' I draw the leather bag from my coat. 'But what is the matter?' There is a suspicious dampness around her eyes.

'It's Amelia!'

'What of her? She left for Bath early this morning. Matthew took her to the Wiltons' house in the trap.'

'She didn't go to Bath. She has run away to London. Look!' She thrusts the book at me, open to a page of agitated writing.

I read in growing horror.

'It is my fault,' she says with great wretchedness. 'She will be ruined and I must go to rescue her. If I can hire a vehicle then maybe I can find her at one of the stops. But I must leave now.'

'On the contrary, it is my fault. If I had told his lordship who and what you were he would have sent you from the house and this would never have happened.'

She glares at me. 'That is very easy for you to say, Harry.'

'I shall come with you.' I go to the door that leads to the servants' staircase and shout down to have the trap made ready.

'I shall do quite well on my own,' she says with a mulish stubbornness.

'No, you will not. I am his lordship's steward and I should not let you go unaccompanied. It is not proper.'

'You're a dreadful driver,' she says.

'Are you better?'

'Actually, yes. I was taught to drive by one of my— by a gentleman.'

'I'm sure you were. Wait here.' I tell Mr Bulmersh and his men to continue with the work and that I am called away upon sudden business, but will return later if I can, or within a day or so. I then dash to my house and throw a few possessions into a bag for the journey, and return to find Sophie seated in the trap, gathering the reins with an air of skill I envy. I toss my bag aboard and clamber up next to her as she clicks her tongue and flicks the whip, and we leave the house in a burst of gravel at a smart canter.

Heaven only knows what will happen in the house while I am gone.

The stage stops at an inn some ten miles away. It will be too late for us to catch Amelia there, for she has a good start of at least an hour, but with luck, and his lordship's horses there (for since he travels frequently to London he keeps horses along the route), we shall overtake it later.

Sure enough, at the inn we find the coach made its stop on time, and a stableman remembers a pretty young woman who travelled alone. We change horses and proceed. We speak little but a few miles further on Sophie reins the horse in.

'He's cast a shoe.'

She jumps down, and lifts the horse's near fore.

'How did you know?'

She gives me an odd look. 'By his gait.' She gathers the reins and knots them out of the way. 'We will lose time, now, for we must get him shod, and we must walk.'

So we set off on foot for the next village, where I hope there is a smithy. As we walk, I become aware that all is not well with Sophie. She coughs occasionally, and blows her nose frequently.

'I fear you're not well, Mrs Marsden.'

'Do not concern yourself, sir.' She regards her limp handkerchief with disgust.

I hand her mine, relatively unused.

We walk on, the horse and Sophie limping (she admits to a blister), for what seems hours. The sun is low in the sky when we see a smudge of smoke on the horizon that indicates a village, and it is almost dusk when we arrive.

There is a smithy, but the smith has closed up shop for the day and gone home to have his dinner. The alehouse, a sorry place with dirty windows and an early customer already asleep on a barrel outside, seems to be the only place that will offer us shelter. The proprietor, impressed by our clothing, I suspect, bows Sophie into a parlour embellished by dead flies on the windowsill while he and I negotiate lodgings for ourselves and the horse for the night.

Sophie

'You said *what*?' I hiss at Harry.

'There is only the one room. Of course I had to say we were married. Your reputation—'

'My reputation? My reputation in Upper Dunghill or whatever the name of this place is?' My indignation is quenched by a sneeze.

'If he thought we were not married he might have refused us shelter. Or charged us more.'

We both fall silent as the waiter, a skinny, unwashed person marginally more filthy than the cloth he carries over one arm, slouches into the parlour to ask if we have finished with our dinner. He casts an acquisitive eye over the aged and undercooked fowl and strange pickled vegetables upon which we have feasted.

'You may bring us tea,' Harry says. 'This time, use boiling water and pray wash the cups in clean water, not that used for washing the cooking pots.'

'Yes, sir.' Slopping gravy, he removes the cover.

'I am not sleeping in the same bed with you,' I say as soon as the waiter has left.

Harry reaches for his travelling chest and flicks it open. An array of bottles stands within. 'I have a tincture which I think you may find effective for your cold, or you can try brandy.'

'Here it would probably poison us.'

'Brandy is brandy. I shall not pay if they have watered it down.'

When the waiter comes back with tea, Harry demands a clean cloth and polishes the cups and tea-spoons with great care. The milk is just beginning to turn, but since I can taste very little I do not really care about the small white blobs floating on the surface.

I retire for bed and a chambermaid, missing a front tooth and with a lank curl of hair hanging from her cap, arrives upstairs to assist with my stays. The bed is none too big, and there is scarcely enough space to accom-modate it, our luggage, and a washstand in the room. Let Harry sleep on the floor, if he can find space. I crawl into bed, aching and miserable, and again in need of a fresh handkerchief. Mine are somewhere in the bottom of my trunk and I lack the energy to retrieve them.

'Mrs Marsden?' Harry thrusts a handkerchief into my hand. 'Sit up, ma'am, I have some brandy for you.'

He places a tallow candle on the washstand. 'Did they use the sheets I brought?'

'I suppose they must have, for they are clean.' I take a swig of brandy. 'Good night, Harry.'

But he does not leave. He moves around the room, finding a bootjack, and I hear the rustling sounds of someone removing garments. I close my eyes. 'I shall not share the bed with you. Can you not sleep in the parlour?'

'I'd rather have you than that greasy waiter as my bedfellow.'

'Oh. Most flattering.' Well, I can see his point. I shift to the far side of the bed, balanced on the edge. 'I trust you'll behave like a gentleman.'

'That has always been my ambition, ma'am.' He sounds amused.

'You know what I mean.' I honk into his handkerchief for emphasis. 'We are merely sharing the bed out of necessity.'

'Ma'am, I am not an animal. I do have some self-control. You need have no fear.'

He climbs into the bed and I feel his legs, bare and hairy, brush against mine. 'What are you wearing?'

'My shirt.'

And I wear a nightgown. Two layers of cotton are all that separate us.

A moment later I shriek, 'Stop it!'

'I would like a little use of the bedclothes, ma'am. May I suggest you do not sleep precisely on the edge of the bed? For in so doing you take the coverings with you.'

'Oh, very well.' With great caution I inch my way

towards the centre of the bed so an equitable arrangement of the bedclothes can be reached.

I lie awake for a little, blowing my nose occasionally. 'Harry?'

'Mmm?'

Good heavens, he is actually going to sleep? How can he? 'She'll be in London by now. I hope she is safe.'

'We'll find her and bring her back home. Never fear.' And he reaches his hand out to clasp mine and squeezes it.

It is a pity it is the hand that holds the sodden handkerchief.

'Goodnight, Mrs Marsden. I hope you feel well in the morning.'

'Goodnight, Mr Bishop.' I wait for him to spring upon me, but his breathing slows and he falls asleep.

So, eventually, do I.

I wake to find him trying to push me out of bed and a brief struggle for supremacy of both bed and covers ensues, both of us half asleep and one of us, at least, in a foul temper and with a sore throat and clogged nose, and the handkerchief nowhere to be found.

'What the devil are you doing?' I croak.

'You're snoring. I'm trying to turn you.'

'What! Nonsense! I never snore.'

'You have a cold. Colds sometimes make people snore.'

'I do not snore. No one has ever complained of it before.' I drag the bedclothes over myself and turn my back on him. As I do so I become aware of an impediment of a somewhat personal nature protruding into my side of the bed. 'Oh, and Harry?'

'Yes?'

'This bed is narrow enough. We cannot afford that sort of thing to take up valuable space.'

'I beg your pardon, ma'am.'

'It is unnatural. I am an *invalid*.' And having had the last word, I wipe my nose on the sheet and compose myself to sleep.

When I wake next it is daylight and Harry, in breeches and shirtsleeves, is shaving. He is a pleasant sight to look upon; he may be slender but he is a well-made man with a certain grace about his person, and if I did not have a cold and he had not accused me of snoring ... I tell myself sternly to cease such thoughts immediately.

'Good morning, Mrs Marsden.' He wipes his face with a towel and dons his spectacles. 'Do you feel well enough to travel?'

'Of course I do.'

'Very well. I'll go downstairs and see about breakfast.' And he puts on coat and waistcoat and strolls from the room.

I ponder his vile accusations of snoring. How on earth

could I have practised my former profession if that were so? (Although little sleeping was involved). Nevertheless I flounce from the bed, even though there is no one to view my performance, and ring the bell several times for the maidservant, who by daylight sports a moustache and a veneer of grime not visible the night before.

When I descend to the parlour Harry is making a hearty breakfast of ham and toast. I drink some tea and eat a piece of toast after examining it for fingerprints. All is set. He has arranged for the horse to be shod and it and the trap returned to the house. We will ride in a vehicle belonging to a gentleman who has business at the next town, a few miles away, where we can pick up the London coach at noon.

Harry rummages in his travelling medicine chest and offers me some salve for my nose, which, I have noticed, glows bright red and is tender to the touch. Upon application I smell faintly of farmyard, for it is tallow with some pungent herbs, but the tenderness is eased. And so we set off once more.

The gentleman who drives us also takes a piglet and a dog, both of which want to become our friends and with whom we share the back of the cart. The piglet, a small black and white creature with delicate hooves and a charming curled tail, has no idea that he will shortly become the dinner of the driver's cousin. He seems altogether too cheerful.

The dog, equally cheerful, sits and scratches most of the time, and I suspect we may carry away some of its fleas.

When we arrive at the coaching inn we find that there are no inside seats to be had.

'What do you think, Mrs Marsden?' Harry says. 'You are not well and I think it likely to rain. I regret I forgot my umbrella.' This last in a shocked whisper that he has succumbed to such a human frailty as forgetfulness.

'Sell you one, sir,' says the young gentleman selling tickets, who chews on the end of his pen, and proceeds to name a ludicrous price for the item he produces, one that barely opens and which was probably abandoned by its former owner. We refuse his generous offer.

The coach arrives with a blast of its horn and passengers tumble out to take advantage of the fifteen minutes it will take to change the horses, scurrying past us into the inn and calling for refreshments. We see our modest luggage loaded, and Harry gallantly assists me on to the roof of the coach where we make ourselves as comfortable as we can. By the afternoon we shall be in London; it is not so long, after all. We set off with a jolt. Our fellow passengers, a group of young men, whoop and shout as though on the hunting field, although their good spirits are dampened by the steady rain that begins to fall.

I unfold the shawl, which for all its delicacy is as strong as iron and tightly woven enough to keep out all but the most severe weather, and wrap it around myself. I steal a glance at Harry, who has turned up his coat collar and sits hunched, hands in pockets. I unfurl the shawl once more.

'Since you bought this you should share it.' I wrap it around us both, bringing us into closer proximity than in the bed we shared last night. We are warm and snug, his thigh against mine, his arm around me beneath the shawl. I rest my head on his shoulder and, despite the lurching of the coach, fall into a deep sleep. I hope I do not snore.

The noise of London wakes me. I am surprised how soon I forgot the din while I was in the country – the rumble of close-packed vehicles, the shouts of street vendors, the noise of a great city as all bustle and go about their business. The rain has stopped, and I am glad of it, for rain in London is a dirty, sooty nuisance.

Perhaps it is my cold that makes me stupid, for I had barely considered what we should do when we arrived in London. I suppose I had some vague idea that we would go door to door from one theatre to another until we found Amelia, but Harry takes charge. He hails a hackney and directs it to, where else, Bishop's Hotel.

Harry

My mother gasps and sinks into a chair – or at least she sinks and I hasten to place a chair strategically for her.

She places a hand on her bosom and gasps for air. 'Tell me you have not been sacked.'

'No, ma'am.'

'Or—' She glances towards the far end of the parlour where Sophie is warming her hands at the fire and whispers, 'Or married?'

'No, ma'am.'

'Oh.' She frowns. 'You know, Harry, it's high time you thought of marriage, for your pa talks more and more of retiring these days, and he's getting tired. You'll need a woman with a head on her shoulders to help you run this place.'

'I doubt Sophie would be interested.'

'That's a great shame.' But she continues, 'And it is just a cold the poor dear young lady suffers from?'

Surely she does not suggest that Sophie is with child!

Sophie, whose hearing is more acute than I had guessed, turns a dazzling smile upon my mother. 'A very slight cold, ma'am. Pray do not be concerned for me. I shall be very well once I am warmed.'

'Oh, my dear Mrs Wallace – I beg your pardon, Harry says I must call you Mrs Marsden now – I cannot hear of Harry dragging you out all over London while you are unwell. You must stay here and we shall take tea and I—'

'I beg your pardon, ma'am, but our business is urgent.' In a few words I tell my mother of Amelia's unfortunate and hasty flight.

'Good Lord, if the girl's not ruined by now, what difference will a few more hours make? Or even another night?' my practical mother cries. 'I insist. You must dine before you go out. Mrs Wallace, I mean Mrs Marsden, we have a nice joint of lamb and some cheese pies and I believe a rocket salad. You are hungry, I'll be bound.'

'Ma'am, you're most kind,' Sophie says. 'Harry – I mean Mr Bishop – I fancy I could eat some dinner. Besides, there'll be no one at any theatre for an hour or so.'

'Well, then! It's all settled. I shall go and see how things are in the kitchen.' My mother grabs my arm and hauls me with her out of the room. 'Why, she looks blooming if a little red around the nose. Have you not made an offer for her yet?' she says as soon as we are out of Sophie's hearing,

'Ma'am, with all due respect, may I suggest you mind your own business.'

She lets out a great shout of laughter and cuffs me around the ear as though I were a boy still. 'I'll wager you gave her the shawl. She keeps it tight around her, but 'pon my honour I'd wager she'd rather it was your arm.'

'She is not well, ma'am.'

My mother winks and heads for the kitchen.

I return to the parlour where Sophie now sits, gazing into the fire.

'Mrs Bishop is right,' she says. 'Amelia is ruined. Our only hope is that we can keep it a secret.'

'Come, maybe it's not so bad.'

'This is the theatre, Harry. Of course it's bad.'

I have a sudden longing to kneel by her and put my arms around her and protect her from the cruelties of the world, but at that moment, my father, having heard that we entertain Mrs Wallace again, comes into the parlour and proceeds to fuss over her.

'Punch!' he announces, and rings the bell. When one of our waiters wanders in, he's told to make haste and bring lemons and hot water and spirits, for my father fancies himself an alchemist of punchmaking. He proceeds to measure and pour and stir amidst clouds of steam, tasting as he goes, purely for Mrs Wallace's – or rather, Mrs Marsden's – health, of course. Sophie drinks a glassful of his fiendish brew and chokes a little, sneezes, and claims it's doing her a world of good. Certainly she looks a little more bright-eyed and more like herself, but she is subdued and I suspect it is not only the cold that dampens her spirits. She must indeed feel responsible for Amelia's escape, but there is something else, too. Does she think of her former lover,

Mr Fordham? Or other former lovers? I wonder if she will take another protector now she is back in London and reminders of her former life are all around. The thought alarms me so much that I gulp a glass of my father's punch and have to sit down, dizzy from the fumes alone.

My father slaps me on the shoulder. For sure, my parents are affectionately heavy-handed today, as over-joyed as they are to see Sophie again, and, to a lesser extent, myself.

To give my mother her due, she excels herself as a hostess, if given to complaining that I look too thin and forcing second and third helpings upon me at dinner, while advising Sophie that she should feed a cold. This inspires a discussion between my parents and eventually the couple of waiters who serve us, as to what feeding a cold in truth means, but Sophie smiles warmly and praises the dinner.

I am much relieved when we can finally tear ourselves from the table and undertake what brought us to London in the first place. My father insists we take the hotel's gig, and my nephew Richard Shilling, who with his father Tom Shilling helped us move Sophie's bed that first time, serves as our driver – for we will need someone to hold the horse while we search the theatres – and so we set off.

'Would you like me to drive, Richard?' Sophie asks as

he drops the whip, tangles the reins, and attempts to drive us into the path of an approaching hackney. 'How is your father? I hope he is well.'

'No, ma'am, that is, thank you kindly, I shall manage.' His voice perambulates a few octaves. He blushes fiercely and his hat falls off. 'And Father is quite well and sends his kind regards, ma'am.'

I jump down from the vehicle to retrieve the hat. God only knows what he'd do if he tried to find it himself – more than likely, he'd hang himself in the harness.

'Richard,' I whisper to him as I hand him his hat, somewhat the worse for wear from the muck of the street, 'she's a female. Your mother is one and I know you have sisters. Mrs Marsden is not related to you but for the purposes of our sanity, may I suggest you think of her as an aunt. Otherwise the gig will become kindling and we in little better condition.'

'Yes, Uncle.' He gazes at his new aunt with pathetic adoration.

She smiles back at him and I grab the reins before they disappear beneath the horse's hooves.

'Drive on, Richard, if you please,' Sophie says with winning sweetness. She turns to me and whispers, 'Why, Harry, he is a worse driver than you. I did not think it possible.'

'You wound me, ma'am.'

Our first stop is at Drury Lane, for Sophie believes

that Amelia, in her *naïveté*, will have tried the best-known theatres first. She leads the way down the narrow alley at the side of the theatre and, telling me to stand aside, has a lively conversation with the doorkeeper.

'Yes, and I'm the Queen of Sheba,' that person announces and bangs the door shut.

She picks her way through the refuse of the alley and returns to my side. 'I told him I was Sophie Wallace and he didn't believe me! I must look a fright. Oh, but wait.'

She darts away and intercepts a pair of gaudily dressed women who approach chattering, and this time I am witness to Sophie's skill as an actress.

She drops a curtsy and launches into a long story about her poor little cousin Amelia – though to be sure, she may go under a different name now, with the prettiest voice, and do they know of her whereabouts? And my, what a handsome bonnet. You won't see anything of that sort in the country. And so on, flattering, cajoling, encouraging them to gossip.

They smile with good humour but tell her there have been no newcomers to the company, not even any hopeful young women who have been turned away recently.

And so it goes for the next few hours until our search must end, for the curtains will be raised now, and this will be Amelia's second night in London. Does she sleep in a doorway somewhere, like the wretches we see on the streets? Or has she been tricked into entering a house of ill repute? A person, particularly a woman, can be engulfed, devoured by the town, sinking into its depths.

'Can you think of nothing you or she said that may tell us where she's gone?'

She shakes her head. 'I told her how I had started with small roles in a lesser company, but Amelia has such certainty in her ability . . .'

'You did badly, ma'am, encouraging her.'

'Preaching does not become you, Harry.'

'Let's drive home, then, Richard.'

Richard flaps the reins on to the horse's back and we leave the fashionable part of town, heading for Aldgate and the hotel. 'I been to a theatre once,' he says.

'Did you, now? What play did you see?' Sophie asks, reducing him to a wreck of embarrassment.

' 'Twasn't a play. Not as such, for it was Easter. There was singing and dancing and a pretty girl in tights.'

'A pantomime?'

'Yes, ma'am. Right near home, too.'

'Near home?' I think for a moment. 'Surely not the Royalty Theatre in Wellclose Square?'

'Maybe, sir.'

'What say you, Sophie? Shall we make one last stop there? It's in the borough of Poplar, quite close to the hotel.'

To my alarm she goes quite pale.

'Is something wrong?' I am afraid she is ill.

'No, no.'

The horse plods through the evening traffic, but as we are going against the general flow we make good progress. I very much doubt the theatre will even be open – it is a disreputable sort of place, not licensed for plays, and generally presents only low forms of entertainment.

We stop in front of the theatre, forlorn-looking and festooned with tattered and shredding posters of past attractions.

'I don't think it's open,' she says. 'Drive on, Richard.'

But one of the large front doors of the theatre is opening as though we are expected and Sophie and I both step down from the trap.

A large burly man wearing a suit of clothes a little too tight, and the skin on his face a little too loose, emerges, moving slowly through the fading light. He extends one fleshy hand to Sophie.

'No!' she cries.

'My little Sophie!' the man says in a sepulchral voice.

'Were you his mistress too?' I am appalled.

'No.' She is so pale her nose appears bright red and dark shadows appear under her eyes. 'No. I murdered him.'

Harry

She murdered him? This disreputable gentleman is certainly no ghost, for he belches loudly and scratches his generous belly.

Sophie grabs for my sleeve and I put my arm around her, for I am afraid she will swoon.

'My darling!' says the dead man. 'Unhand my betrothed, sir.'

I push past him, supporting Sophie in my arms, and into the theatre. The doors to the auditorium stand open and there seems to be some sort of activity on the stage, a boy turning cartwheels, and a group of people banging scenery around.

I help Sophie on to one of the wooden benches.

Someone rushes at me and grabs me by the collar, sending my hat flying. 'What the devil are you doing with her?'

I must be in a madhouse. I push the second

gentleman away, and find myself face to face with the first, who gazes at Sophie with inane sentimentality. 'My little flower,' he croons.

'Your betrothed?'

'In a manner of speaking, sir, yes. She is my sun, my joy and hope.'

'She is not, sir, and she is certainly not yours. Yes, sir, what may I do for you?' For the other gentleman approaches, fists clenched in a pugilistic, fierce sort of way.

'Take your hands from my child!'

His child?

'Oh, Pa,' says a weak voice from around the level of my chest, 'do hold your tongue.'

'She lives!' Mr Marsden cries, for indeed that is who he must be, and now I see the similarity of bone and colouring, the same fine eyes, that he shares with Sophie.

'Of course I live, Pa. The wonder is that Mr Sloven does. I thought I'd killed him. And as for you, Pa, where the devil have you been?'

He lays his hand on his breast. 'My child, restored to me! A most profitable and healthful tour, my dear, Portsmouth, Southampton, salubrious spots by the sea. And then we ran out of money and returned, and Mr Sloven, since you are affianced, is kind enough to finance our thespian endeavours here.'

'I am not affianced to Mr Sloven.'

'Ah. I see,' says her fond parent and turns to me. 'You keep company with my daughter, sir? She's fond of a pretty bonnet, you know. I doubt she'll stay long if you can't afford better than that. Why, Sophie, I'm sorry to see you come down in the world so.'

'There's nothing wrong with my bonnet. I'm a respectable woman, sir. And I'm certainly not engaged to Mr Sloven.'

'But, Sophie, my love—' Sloven flings himself with a thud on to his knees, his pudgy frame trembling. 'Sophie, was it not here we plighted our troth?'

'You put your lecherous hands all over me, you mean. And then I hit you.' She sits up and glares at us all.

'True, I fear.' Jake Sloven sighs. 'Yet in that moment, like Paul upon the road to Damascus, I became a changed man. A white light shone about me and angel voices told me, "She is yours. Sophie Wallace is yours and will return to your bosom." And so I have waited for you.' He spreads his arms wide.

'I regret I have no intention whatsoever of returning to your bosom.' She unties her bonnet strings. 'I did my very best to avoid your bosom and the rest of you too, Sloven.'

'Not even to give your poor old father the chance for theatrical glory?' Mr Marsden looks somewhat concerned.

'Not even for that. Why didn't you tell me where you'd gone, Pa?'

He draws himself up. 'I hadn't seen you for six months, my dear. Your old Pa wasn't good enough for you. I was wounded, here in my heart.' He strikes his chest.

'You know why, Pa. Charlie was forever gazing into your actresses' bosoms.' She glares at Sloven, who is doing that exact same thing to her, and gets to her feet.

'But come to your father's arms, my child! Let me embrace thee!' Despite his theatricality, I see some genuine affection between Marsden and his daughter.

Suspecting this happy reunion may be protracted, I go outside to tell Richard to take the horse home. We can walk the half-mile or so to the hotel.

When I return another personage has joined the group, a beautiful woman with dark curls tumbling down her back, flashing eyes, and a figure of generous proportions spilling from a spangled satin gown. Her skirts are hoisted to reveal pink tights and soft leather boots. Her beauty is enhanced and made even more extraordinary by a luxuriant black beard that spills upon her superb bosom. Hands on hips, she gazes upon the embracing father and daughter with deep suspicion.

Marsden extricates himself from his daughter's arms. 'Ah, my dear. This is my daughter, Sophie.'

'Your daughter!' She looks her up and down, lip curling. 'Oh, of course she's your daughter. I know you, Billy Marsden. Just like that niece you have backstage.'

'Ma'am.' I bow to her. 'May I introduce Mrs Sophie Wallace. She is indeed Mr Marsden's daughter.'

'That's never Sophie Wallace! Not the most notorious woman in London – or as of two months ago.' She strokes her beard. 'And who are you, sir? The Prince of Wales?'

'Harry Bishop. Your servant, ma'am.'

'Hmm.'

Sophie holds out her hand. 'I'm most pleased to meet you.'

'Yes, my dear,' Marsden says, 'Fatima, the Bearded Woman of Constantinople. I pray you will learn to love her and call her Mama.'

'Sylvia Cooper of Wapping, in real life,' she says. She looks upon Sophie with a somewhat less suspicious eye.

'You should see her on the trapeze!' Mr Marsden continues. 'She is a goddess, revered by all. Such grace, such ease, such perfection of limbs . . .'

'Ballocks. They want to see my thighs and my beard. I'll fetch us some drink.'

'A lovely girl,' Marsden sighs as he watches her depart. 'The beard took some getting used to, I must admit, but she has a heart of gold. Of gold, sir. Speaking of which . . .' He casts an anxious glance at Sloven. 'It is his word against yours, you know, Sophie my dear, and if you are not engaged, you will see your pa begging in the streets.'

'Oh, nonsense.'

Sophie

I suppose I should be flattered that Harry Bishop looks so very out of sorts at the appearance of Jake Sloven; I am certainly out of sorts, in particular at the suggestion that Mr Sloven and I have some sort of understanding. First he appeared like a ghost – a moment I am sure Amelia would have appreciated, for it was positively Shakespearian – and frightened me to death, and then to tell my father that he and I are engaged! I almost wish the blow with the piece of scenery had been more effective.

And my father has a mistress with a beard. Well, that is odd, but she seems more pleasant than other ladies he has associated with. His choice in ladies, bearded or otherwise, is not my chief concern at the moment; I fear he has sold me to Mr Sloven to pursue pantomimes in this theatre.

Sylvia, true to her word, has returned with bottles and glasses, assisted by the boy who turned cartwheels upon the stage.

'You have a cold, my dear,' my fond parent pronounces. 'I do not wish your ill humours to infect my players. Pray keep a little apart from me.'

'Pa,' I say, backing off as far as I can but still within whispering distance, 'pray tell me what arrangement you have made with Jake Sloven concerning my person.'

'My dear! You do not accuse me of pandering, I hope.'

'I hope not, too, Pa.' I wonder what Harry is about and look round to see him gazing at Sylvia and her beard with profound admiration.

'The thing is, my petal, I would not have counted Sloven as one of my intimate acquaintances until a month or so ago. He suffered some sort of mishap and had his head bound up for a few days and emerged from his suffering a changed man; and, according to him, an engaged man, and engaged to you. The last thing he remembered before his fall was your acceptance of his advances. Naturally, I gave my consent, a formality only, for you are of age. I was surprised.' My father glances at Sloven's unlovely person. 'He is perhaps not the most handsome of fellows, but he has a good heart, and you, my dear, should settle down, eh? No more gallivanting around in the height of fashion on the arms of your sprigs of the nobility, not at your advanced age.'

'I am nine and twenty, sir!'

'Precisely.'

I sink on to a bench, my head in my hands. 'I do not believe this, Pa.'

'Well, think about it, my dear. With your fall from grace – not precisely grace, I should say rather your fall from fashion – you may find your future uncertain. Why, I haven't seen a mention of you in the newspapers for weeks. What have you been up to?'

'I've been in the country. I have been a teacher of singing.'

'Have you now!' He regards me with paternal pride. 'And why did you return?'

I shrug and decide to entrust him with the whole sorry story – I leave out the more lurid details of my association with Harry – and he shakes his head.

'Dear, dear,' he intones. 'You should not imagine, my child, that every gentleman you meets pursues you. And who did, in fact, give you the shawl?'

'Mr Bishop.' Despite my whisper, that gentleman looks my way at the mention of his name.

'He is an admirer, then?'

'Yes. No. I don't know. He proposed and I turned his offer down.'

'At your age and with your reputation, my dear, you should not be so precipitate, yet since you have another suitor, indeed are all but married, it is just as well. I'll tell Sloven we shall call the banns, then.'

'No!' But seeing my father's look of dejection, I add, 'Give me time to accustom myself to the idea, Pa. I don't want to do anything to upset your financial arrangements, but I'm quite sure I don't want to marry Sloven.'

'I assure you, he will grow on you.'

I fall silent at the unpleasant images that come to my mind. For sure, Sloven had achieved a high degree of unpleasantness all on his own, but this new, reformed

Sloven, the sentimental, sighing, adoring Sloven who gazes at me like a hungry spaniel – I do not want him, or any part of him, growing in any way in my presence.

'But I have another surprise for you, my dear,' my fond parent says. 'Come with me. There is someone you must meet.'

'You have sold me to yet another gentleman?'

'Sharper than a serpent's tooth!' my father cries. 'Oh, Sophie, how you pierce my heart.'

'You might have a little more concern for mine before selling me to the highest bidder.' Not a quarter hour in his company and already I am exasperated by my theatrical sire.

He casts a look of deep sorrow at me that does not affect me in the least. 'Mr Bishop, sir, if you please, you should accompany us.'

Harry, receiving a juggling lesson, looks up at the sound of his name, and wooden balls fall and roll on the floor around him.

'Now look what you've done, Billy,' says Sylvia. 'And he was doing so well.'

My father leads us backstage, rubbing his hands together with glee.

'What is he about?' Harry asks me in a whisper as we cross the stage. He has assessed my father and found him wanting, and I am infuriated that Harry should do so (while agreeing with his verdict).

I shrug. I think longingly of punch and a fireside and Mrs Bishop fussing over me, and a clean handkerchief.

'And, behold!' My father flings open a door.

Amelia sits darning stockings. When she sees us she jumps to her feet with a cry of joy and flings herself into my arms.

14

Sophie

'Oh, you're safe. Thank God.' And then relief gives way to anger and tears from us both. 'How could you do this, you foolish, foolish girl? We have been worried half to death over you.'

'Forgive me. I am so sorry, Mrs Marsden. I know it was a mistake and I have been so lucky. I know now how wrong I was.' She draws away from me. 'How did you find me?'

'Pure chance.' In the one theatre in London I had hoped to avoid. 'And you left behind your diary.'

She blushes, affronted. 'Some of that was very private.'

'But how did you arrive here?' Harry says.

'It's very simple,' Amelia says. 'On the journey to London, I found a newspaper, only a couple of days old, at one of the inns and read that Mr Marsden planned a new production in the Theatre Royal in Poplar. So I made my way here and told Mr Marsden that I knew you, Mrs Marsden. I did not realize you were father and daughter.'

Indeed, no. Why should she? I had told her myself Billy Marsden and I were only distantly related and at this moment I wish it were so.

I turn on my father. 'And you did not think to send word to anyone?'

'These are the thanks I get? She is perfectly safe here and proves herself a treasure. And such a pretty singing voice. She will be an asset to the company.' My father beams upon her. 'Is this not a delightful surprise for you? She has told me all about you, and we have been expecting you. Why, but an hour or so ago we sent word to Bishop's Hotel – a fine establishment, sir – that if anyone came seeking Miss Amelia, they were to come here directly.'

'An hour ago!' I cry.

'I would not tell him where I came from before,' Amelia says. 'Does Lord Shad know? I fear he will be angry.'

'Not yet,' Harry says. 'Someone, Miss Amelia, must tell him.'

I turn on him. 'If anyone other than we three know of this she will be ruined.'

'But— but I intend to stay here,' Amelia says. 'Mrs Marsden, this is what I want to do and you as much as suggested I should become an actress.'

Harry looks at me, eyebrows raised, and then back at Amelia. 'You are Lord Shad's ward, Miss Amelia. I am his lordship's trusted servant and I should be derelict in my duties if I were to let you remain here. Mrs Marsden, I trust you do not suggest we lie to Lord Shad.'

'If necessary, yes.'

'I regret it has nothing to do with you, Mrs Marsden. You are no longer a member of the household.'

'Miss Amelia, your guardian does not know you are here?' my father says. 'Dear, dear. This is not well done. I shall have to send you back home, you wicked girl.' But he smiles as he says it.

'I will not go.' Amelia sits down in her chair and picks up her discarded darning.

'What else have you done while you were here?' I ask.

'Yesterday I hemmed costumes,' she says with great pride.

'And has Mr Marsden offered you a contract? Or any money?'

She shakes her head.

'Think of it as an apprenticeship in the theatre, my dear,' my father says. 'After all, Sylvia and I are supplying room and board, and that counts for something. You, my dear Sophie, spent years absorbing the art of the stage along with your mother's milk – that woman of blessed memory, ah, how I miss her – and this is much the same.'

'Oh, certainly, except that she is not your daughter and apprentices have a contract and some protection. How are we to know you do not expect Miss Amelia to darn your stockings for the next ten years?'

'My dear, I think I have an eye, nay a gift for nurturing young talent. Why, she reminds me so of you when you were a girl, Sophie!' He lays a paternal hand on Amelia's head and she beams up at him.

'Indeed? You intend to sell her when she is past her prime so you may stage a pantomime?'

'Sophie, that was unworthy of you.' My father heaves a sigh. 'This child will in time progress to a small role and then greater roles, and meanwhile she learns about the theatre under the tender care of Sylvia and myself. And Sophie, if you would not mind, pray remember Amelia is my niece, for Sylvia is of a somewhat jealous temperament, and I value the peace of hearth and home. Or of our lodgings, rather.'

Harry says, 'Mr Marsden, Amelia must come with us. She is a member of the family of Viscount Shadderly, related to the Earl of Beresford, and it is most improper for her to be here.'

'Shadderly . . . Beresford. Well, well. Are either of those two gentlemen interested in the theatre, Mr Bishop?'

I answer for him, recognizing the avarice in my

father's eyes. 'No, they are not. His lordship is certainly not interested in seeing his ward on the stage or being employed in a dubious capacity in the theatre. She has signed no agreement, Pa. You can't keep her here.' To Amelia I say, 'Perhaps Mr Marsden omitted to mention that this theatre is not licensed to perform plays. He will have you, at best, in tights and performing in a pantomime.'

'But Mr Marsden said . . .' Amelia looks from me to my father and back to me. 'Mrs Marsden, you said I was good enough to sing and act professionally.'

'Well, there you are!' murmurs my dear papa.

'I did not say that exactly. I said with application and hard work you would be as good as anyone on the London stage. I certainly did not intend you to take this most unwise step, to run from those who love you and who have your wellbeing at heart. And for what? Not to become a respected Shakespearian actress, but to perform in low comedy . . .' I stop, seeing the contempt on Harry's face; he thinks I encouraged Amelia to take this rash action and I fear I may well have filled her head with all sorts of fanciful notions. Did I not advise her that one could be an actress and a lady too?

'We are upsetting the young lady,' my father says. 'Come, Sophie, my dear, the hour of twilight, that time of fairies and ghosts and magic, is almost upon us and the cost of candles is something shocking. Mr Bishop must advise Miss Amelia on the best course of action.' He sighs. 'To see such a treasure slip through my hands! It is hard, my dear Sophie, very hard.'

We all return to the stage, a strange procession indeed. Amelia clasps her darning as though it was a playbook for one of Shakespeare's tragic roles, Harry close beside her, avoiding my gaze. To my surprise I see Richard is in the auditorium, staring around him with the look of delight and horror that those unaccustomed to the theatre wear when they view it at any other time than during a performance.

'Uncle Harry!' He approaches, hat in hand, and his nervousness has gone. Although he has the shocked appearance of a rabbit at the approach of a large and hungry dog, he is quite calm and steady. 'Sir, Uncle, you must come home.'

'What's happened? I thought I told you to go back to the hotel.'

'I did, sir, and they sent me to get you.' He swallows. 'It's bad, sir. Very bad.'

'My mother?' Harry says in a shocked whisper.

Richard shakes his head and Harry straightens his shoulders and addresses my father. 'You sent word to the hotel with the address for your lodgings, Marsden? Very good. I shall call upon you and Miss Amelia as soon as I am able to. Your servant.' He bows, ever correct.

My father nudges me. 'Go with him, girl. He needs

you, it's as plain as the nose on your face.'

I take a step towards Harry, but he turns a look upon me of such contempt that I fear what he will say or do if I come any nearer. He inclines his head in the approximation of a bow and leaves with Richard.

'Well!' my father says, rubbing his hands. 'What did you do to that nice young man, Sophie? For you've injured him, 'tis plain to see.'

'He blames me for Amelia's escape to London, Pa.'

'I thought he had more sense than that.'

'Well, chances are he'll be sacked now, and that's my fault for sure. I asked him to come with me to find her, and he knew who I was when I arrived at the house and he did not reveal my identity to the family. He blames himself for that, that I am a corrupting influence.'

'Nonsense!' my father says. 'What, you, a corrupting influence? Of course he could have told Lord Shad who you were and he didn't, and I think I know the reason why.'

'No.' I shake my head. 'You are mistaken, Pa.' I lean my head against his shoulder for what comfort my father affords, for I find I am sorely in need of it, weary and sick at heart.

My nose is stuffed up and I should like to retire to bed. 'Amelia, my dear, would you mind if I went back to the hotel?'

She smiles. 'Of course you should, Sophie. Mr Bishop

would like to have you there, I am sure, if there is some sort of family trouble. And Mrs Marsden, I am indeed sorry I have put you and Mr Bishop to all this trouble. You have both been so good to me. Please thank him from me.'

'I shall. And I am so glad you are safe.'

'I like your papa very much,' she says. 'He has been very kind.'

Well, of course she does, poor child, bereft of the father she thought she had, and horrified to learn of her real sire. Even Billy Marsden seems a paragon of parenthood compared to the wicked old Viscount.

I bid my father a fond farewell and set off for the hotel, a scant half-mile walk.

When I arrive, I find a coach has just arrived and is disgorging passengers who throng inside, ordering food and drink. I am relieved that at least the building has not burned down. Mr Bishop, though, is not in the yard to welcome guests; instead one of the waiters is there performing that role.

I enter the building too, and find my way to the private quarters of the inn, where I tap on the door of the family's parlour.

A woman with floating dark hair and deep brown eyes answers, signs of weeping upon her face. 'This part of the hotel is not open to guests, ma'am.'

'I'm Sophie Wallace.'

'Oh.' She looks at me with sudden comprehension. There's something about her that reminds me of Harry; the sharp cheekbones and something in the shape of the jaw, perhaps. 'Ma's spoken of you.'

'Are you Harry's sister?'

She nods. 'I'm Mary Shilling. You've met my husband and son, I believe.'

'I don't wish to intrude, but may I be of some assistance to you?'

She attempts to smile. 'You're very kind, Mrs Wallace. My father is grievously ill of an apoplexy. The surgeon is with him now.'

'Is that Sophie?' a voice cries from the room behind Mrs Shilling.

'Yes, Ma.'

'Well, let her come in.' But Mrs Bishop's voice lacks its usual vibrancy and is hoarse as if she too has wept.

Mary opens the door and I enter. Mrs Bishop sits upon the sofa, tears spilling from her eyes. 'My dear Sophie,' she cries. 'I was hoping you would come.'

'Mrs Bishop, I am so very sorry.'

'Will you sit with us a little, my dear? Mary, pray pour Sophie some tea. Harry will be glad you are here.'

I doubt it, but take her hand.

'Mr Bishop was here, taking some tea with me,' she says, and I know it is a story she will repeat over and over in disbelief as the reality of her loss sinks home. 'He said to me, "Mrs Bishop, you look most handsome today," and then a strange expression came over his face.

'I said, "What is wrong, my dear? You do not look quite the thing."

'And he started to say something and dropped like a stone, here.' She points to the floor. 'Like a felled tree. It was a dreadful thing to see. And I knelt by him and took his hand and said, "Peter, my dear" – for it is only under the most intimate of circumstances that I use his Christian name – "you must speak to me." But his hand was cold, cold as a stone, and I called the girl for hot bricks but he said not a word more to me and did not open his eyes again.' She falls silent, biting her lip. 'I wonder what it was he tried to tell me. Why did he leave me so?'

'He's not gone yet, Ma,' Mrs Shilling says. She hands me a cup of tea and sits down next to Mrs Bishop. 'The surgeon said he has known some in these cases rally. We'll see what he says when he and Harry come back downstairs.'

So we wait, and after a while, a gentleman who must be the surgeon and Harry come into the room, their faces grave.

Harry looks at me with mild surprise but he appears dazed, as though he might expect to see any number of people or things upon the sofa and not be much moved. I rise and stand aside, and watch as Harry takes his mother's hands and speaks quietly to her.

She wails and shakes her hands free, saying no, it cannot, must not be, while Mrs Shilling embraces her and the two women rock to and fro.

'You should go and speak to him, Ma,' Harry says. 'He might hear you. Your voice will comfort him.'

She nods and she and Mrs Shilling leave the room for the bedchamber where Harry's father lies dying.

Harry exchanges a few words with the surgeon and tugs on a bellrope. One of the female servants of the hotel, pale and as red-eyed as her mistress, is summoned to bring the surgeon's hat and gloves, and Harry and I are left alone.

'I am so very sorry, Harry.'

He nods. He looks older, sombre, and his shoulders droop as though intolerable burdens have been placed upon him, and indeed, so they have. 'I must write to my other sisters and brother. God knows when the letters will reach them. We last had word from Joseph some six months ago when his ship was in port. My sister, the one who is a housekeeper, is in Yorkshire, and Eliza in Bristol expects her third child any day. There is not time for . . .' He blinks at me and takes off his spectacles, rubbing them absently on his cuff. 'Thank you for keeping my mother and sister company, Mrs Wallace.'

I have not been addressed as Mrs Wallace in such a while that I start at the use of my name.

'I beg your pardon. Mrs Marsden, then. I have

another favour to beg of you, ma'am, that you will stay with my mother and sister this night.'

'Of course.'

He continues, 'I must write also to Lord Shad, to . . . pray God no one in the neighbourhood knew of Amelia's departure. Her reputation may yet be saved. But . . .' he looks at me, confused. 'I regret this delays our departure for Brighton.'

'Harry, sit. You should drink some tea.'

He does so and sits stirring his tea like a man in a dream, but when he drinks it he becomes more like himself. I wish I could touch him and give him some human comfort, but I know too that his formality, his wish for order, is the only protection he can offer his family.

'The physician says he doubts my father will last the night,' he says and then falls silent again.

I go upstairs to the bedchamber where Harry's father lies, attended by his wife and daughter, only the slight rise and fall of his chest indicating that he lives still.

Richard, solemn and somehow less gawky, as though he has grown up in the past couple of hours, is summoned to bid his grandfather farewell, and both he and his father Thomas weep.

Harry returns from his letter writing and sits beside his sister in silence, his arm around her shoulders.

Mrs Bishop holds her husband's hand and talks of

how things go at the hotel this night and how the cook, in her grief, burned some chickens and drank a quart of porter; of compliments the hotel has received from guests; and how those who have stayed there before wish Mr Bishop well. Mrs Bishop tells him she has no doubt Mr Bishop will rally and that she will nurse him back to health and take him away for a holiday, for in all this time he has never had one. Sea air, she thinks, would do him good. She holds his hand to her face, talking of the bright sparkle of sunlight on sea, the slap and tug of waves, the cries of seagulls as they ride the winds overhead.

Gradually her voice becomes quieter and I think she talks of their courtship, of their years together, and of their children and grandchildren.

Clocks strike, coaches arrive and depart, and the night watchmen call the hours and announce that it is a fine night.

So it may be, but not for the Bishop family. Shortly before dawn Mr Bishop dies.

I leave the family so they may grieve alone and find the hotel staff at the bottom of the stairs, waiting, many of them in tears. They don't need me to tell them what has happened, but they look to their new master, for Harry has followed me downstairs.

'My father and your master Mr Bishop is dead.' His voice is quiet and kind. 'I thank you all for your concern.

The Norwich coach arrives in fifteen minutes, so make sure all is ready. Bring Mrs Bishop some tea in the parlour, if you please.' He turns to me. 'May I ask you to stay with my mother? She should sleep. I'll have a room made up for her. Mary must return home to her children.'

I cannot refuse. When Mrs Bishop comes back downstairs, a woman having arrived to lay the corpse out, she is in a state of nervous agitation, scarcely able to keep still, and then collapsing into tears. She talks incoherently of her dead husband and what is to become of her now.

She grips my arm during one of these panicked ramblings. 'You must help Harry. He will need a wife now. We always meant for him to run the hotel, but not yet. Not so soon. Promise me, Sophie.'

I urge her to calm herself.

'Has he made you an offer?' she asks with something of her former bright-eyed energy.

'He did, ma'am.'

'Oh, thank God.' But then she sees my expression. 'You refused him, my dear Sophie? How could this be? But never mind, he will propose again, and this time you must accept.'

'Ma'am, I regret I—'

'Promise me!'

'If he asks, I shall consider it,' I say carefully. She is

not to know how unlikely it is he would ask me again.

I cannot tell her that her son has lost all regard, all respect for me, for I think I would weep myself if I were to tell her.

But my answer seems to satisfy her for she calms a little and drinks some tea, finally allowing me to help her to a bedchamber and assist her in going to bed.

'This was the room Harry slept in as a boy,' she says. 'He and our other son, Joseph. You see here, they measured themselves and marked it on the doorjamb.'

Sure enough, a series of notches, one headed by an H and the other with a J, measure the growth of the Bishop sons.

'Harry was so angry that Joseph was always taller.' She manages a smile. 'My dear, you will like him so much when you meet him, and my other daughters Sara and Eliza. To think they never bid their papa goodbye!'

She argues very little when I suggest she take some laudanum and she falls asleep.

I go to my bedchamber and lie on my bed, thinking I shall sleep only a little while, but when I awaken it is late afternoon. Outside I hear a coach horn and the clop of hooves and the rumble of vehicles on the cobbled yard of the inn. When I go to the window I see Harry, wearing a long apron, greeting passengers as his father did, a black armband on one sleeve. He smiles and makes conversation and I marvel that he is able to do so with such ease; a few, noting the symbol of mourning, stop and converse more deeply with him or shake his hand.

A familiar trio enter the courtyard on foot – my father, Sylvia, and Amelia. I smooth my skirts and splash a little water on my face and go downstairs to meet them.

15

Sophie

'A dreadful business, Mr Bishop. Dreadful indeed.'
My father dabs at his eyes with a large
handkerchief he wields like a theatrical prop, which is
exactly what it is. 'Your late father was well known and
deeply respected in the neighbourhood. It is a loss, sir.
An inconsolable loss for us all. My commiserations, sir.'
He wrings Harry's hand.

'For heaven's sake, Pa, you didn't even know him,' I
mutter to my sire and pull him aside.

The last of the arrivals have entered the hotel, and
Harry invites us into the family's parlour, where Mrs
Shilling and Mrs Bishop preside over the teapot. A few
other ladies, who are introduced as friends of the family,
gaze in astonishment at Sylvia's beard and then talk
loudly of the weather.

Mrs Bishop, swathed in black like a mourning queen,
graciously accepts the condolences of the newcomers,

although somewhat taken aback at my father's florid eloquence. She barely seems to notice Sylvia's beard and smiles faintly at Amelia's youthful prettiness.

After a while, Harry enters, his apron discarded. He announces his mother must rest, and with great tact and firmness directs the visitors out, but asks me and Amelia to stay.

Now everyone has gone he looks weary, like an actor coming off the stage, and so it has been for him, I suppose, as he maintains the friendly pleasant façade of the hotel keeper.

He sinks into a chair and accepts a cup of tea. I wish I could offer him more, some kindness or words of comfort, for now he looks weary and sad.

Amelia produces a needle and thread from her pocket and stitches at a loose ribbon on her bonnet.

'Your bonnet turned out well,' I say as she bites off the thread.

'Oh, had you not seen it finished before?'

I shake my head. She had worked at that bonnet last week. Was she thinking even then of running away to London?

'Mrs Henney admired it, too. I bought the ribbons from her.'

'When did Mrs Henney see it?' Harry sits bolt upright.

'Why, just before I boarded the coach to London.'

'*What?*'

'Why do you look at me like that, Mr Bishop?' She looks at me for reassurance. 'Mrs Marsden, I met her while I was waiting for the coach. She drove up in her donkey cart and offered me a lift while I waited at the crossroads, but I told her I did not need one.'

'So she knew you were going to London? Alone?' I ask.

'Yes, but I did not tell her why, for it was none of her business.'

'What did she and you talk about?' Harry asks.

'Oh, very little. She teased me that I had a lover waiting in London and of course I told her she was mistaken. She very kindly offered to wait with me until the coach arrived.' She gazes at us both. 'Did I do something wrong?'

'Amelia, my dear, Mrs Henney is the biggest gossip in Norfolk.' I break the truth to her as gently as I can. 'Your only hope, to retain your reputation, was that no one but us should know of your escapade. Now everyone – the village and all the surrounding families with whom Lord Shad wished you to be known as an equal – will know that you are ruined.'

'Ruined!' She stares at me in horror. 'What shall I do?'

Harry puts his teacup down and stands. 'We must take you to Brighton as soon as we can so you may throw yourself on Lord Shad's mercy. I doubt whether he knows any of this and it is best he hears it first from you. We bury my father tomorrow.' He says it with no emotion, no inflexion in his voice at all, but his hands are clenched tight. 'Meanwhile, you and I must talk, Miss Amelia. I'll escort you back to your lodgings. Mrs Marsden, I should be obliged if you will stay here until my return in case my mother requires your company.'

'Cannot Mrs Marsden accompany us?'

'No, Miss Amelia, she cannot.'

He bows, and I can only admire the eloquence of Mr Bishop's bows, for this one expresses a lofty officiousness that makes me grit my teeth. As he escorts Amelia from the parlour, she sends me an agonized, tearful glance.

I sit in the parlour as the light fades, wondering if I should move into the lodgings with Amelia and my father as I find the proximity to Harry disturbing and painful, but I do not want to leave Mrs Bishop. As I bend to light a candle at the fireplace, Mary Shilling enters the room again.

'Where is Harry?'

'He is escorting Amelia back to her lodgings.'

'Oh. Mrs Marsden, Sophie, may I ask the favour of you staying with us tomorrow? My father will be buried and we women shall be here. We should so like your company; you are a great comfort to us and Harry is . . . well, I need not tell you of Harry's opinion.'

Oddly she too seems to think Harry holds me in great esteem. Doubtless she and her mother have been planning further attempts to make me the mistress of Bishop's Hotel.

Harry, when he returns, looks even more strained and worried than he did before. He dons his apron. I watch him square his shoulders and assume a welcoming smile for the next group of travellers and wish I could ease his burden, but I cannot. I have assisted his family because I like them and I feel for them in their sorrow; I have become close to his mother in particular, even if she continues in the belief that I am to marry her son. I am willing for her to make that assumption if it gives her some comfort, although I know my refusal (or more likely his disinclination to make me a second offer) will sadden her. But I must leave Bishop's Hotel soon, to become the drudge in my father's company if I can do so without fulfilling any obligation to Sloven; and if that is unavoidable, I shall go elsewhere.

The next day is that of the funeral and for the first time in living memory, Bishop's Hotel closes its doors for the morning. Mrs Bishop, Mary Shilling, and other female friends and relatives listen in the parlour to the tread of the undertakers' feet on the staircase as they take the coffin downstairs. Harry and Thomas Shilling are two of the pall-bearers, as is my father, who weeps into another black-edged handkerchief the size of a tablecloth. The stable yard is deserted except for the carriage with two black and plumed horses.

Mrs Bishop wails and presses her palm against the window as though trying to touch her husband one last time.

The coffin is loaded into the carriage, and the male staff of the hotel flock into the stable yard, sombre, some weeping, all of them wearing black armbands. They gather behind Harry and the procession sets off, Mrs Bishop watching as it leaves the yard, her forehead pressed against the glass. None of us dare to disturb her.

'What shall we do?' Amelia whispers to me, for she and Sylvia have come to join the mourning women.

'Nothing,' I whisper back. 'She will let us know when she is ready.'

Finally she moves. 'Fetch some claret,' she says, and the maidservants scurry to do her bidding.

'But, Cousin—' remonstrates a female relative. 'It is not proper.'

'My Peter liked a glass of claret, God bless him, and if you don't like it, Cousin Letitia, you may leave.'

'Well!' Cousin Letitia and the pale, skinny child who is either her daughter or servant, I cannot tell which, leave, noses in the air.

I regret to say we all get drunk as not one, but many bottles of claret are produced from the cellar, but the atmosphere improves considerably. A hectic jollity reigns. Stories concerning childbirth, husbands' antics in the bedchamber and elsewhere, and other female matters are exchanged, and Mrs Bishop weeps a little still, but she laughs occasionally too. Amelia blushes quite pink at what she hears but she pays close attention.

A cough comes from the doorway. Sylvia, who has been juggling empty bottles, scoops them up into her arms, and several of the ladies, who have raised their petticoats to take advantage of the fire, for it is a rainy, chilly day, make themselves decent.

Harry stands there, sniffing a half-full glass of wine. 'For God's sake, Ma, that's the good claret.'

'Of course it is. Your father would have wished it.'

'Of course he would have. Will all the ladies stay to dinner?'

The ladies indicate they should like to indeed, and assure Harry that even the two among us who have fallen asleep will wish to dine.

Harry smiles and sneezes. 'Mrs Marsden, I should like a word with you, if you please.'

'Certainly,' I say with a bravado inspired by the wine. Surely he is not going to make me an offer now?

He offers his arm and takes me into the office opposite the kitchen, where he hangs his hat on a peg on the door.

'Mrs Marsden,' he says with great formality, and I wait for him to drop to one knee.

Instead he sneezes again.

'Oh, Harry, I am sorry. Did you catch my cold?'

'I fear so. It is nothing.'

'I hope you are right. I am almost better now.'

'I am glad to hear it.'

But he looks unwell, tired and strained, pale except for a redness around the eyes, his voice hoarse. He continues, 'As you have realized, I must manage Bishop's Hotel now. It is something my parents expected me to do, and while I did not anticipate taking on the responsibility for some years, circumstances have . . .' He pauses and reaches out his hand to touch the pipe that lies on the desk; his father's pipe, a finely turned piece of ivory and wood. He stands absolutely still.

I lay my hand on his arm.

'So.' He shakes my hand off, not in an unkind way, but rather in an absent-minded way, as though I was a fly that had alighted on his sleeve. 'I know my duty. You may have noticed that my mother expects me to marry, for this sort of establishment is best run by husband and wife . . .'

He spoils the effect of his eminently practical speech by producing a handkerchief and blowing his nose very loudly.

'Of course you should marry!' I cry with a little too much enthusiasm.

'Well, then.' He picks up the pipe and lays it carefully

aside. 'I think you understand me.'

This is a proposal? From Harry Bishop who kissed (and more) like a fallen angel?

'Ye-es,' I respond with some hesitation in my voice.

'It will be best all round, I think.'

'Of course.' I look at him but he's not looking at me. He's started stacking papers together. 'When shall you tell Mrs Bishop?'

'Oh, soon. But first I must accompany Miss Amelia to Brighton and talk with Lord Shad.'

I give an inappropriate and nervous giggle. 'Oh, of course. Well, that is . . .' I had almost forgotten about Amelia. How foolish of me. 'So when should we go to Brighton?'

'We?'

'Well, naturally I should accompany you. And I should apologize to Lord Shad for my lapse in judgement regarding Amelia's ambitions.'

'I don't believe that will be absolutely necessary, Mrs Marsden. You did give notice, after all.' He starts on another pile of papers. 'Oh, good lord, more bills.'

'But— but I'd like to see the family again.' For as an engaged woman I will have immediate respectability should we meet anyone from my former life. 'I think Amelia would like to have me with her. I know she will be nervous about seeing Lord Shad again under the circumstances.'

He stops his perusal of the bills. 'Yes, I believe you have a point there. And it would be more proper if she had the company of an older female.'

'Not very gallant, sir.'

He blows his nose again in reply.

'Harry, you really don't sound well. May I fetch you something for your cold?'

'No, no, Mrs Marsden.' Is that irritation I hear in his voice? Well, I have not received a proposal in some years, other than Harry's last incompetent attempt, so maybe I have forgotten how it was done. Also he is unwell and moreover has just buried his dear papa, and possibly he is concerned about my suitability as his helpmeet in running the hotel. He has a lot on his mind, it is true.

'Who shall run the hotel in your absence?' I wish to show him that I am a practical woman.

'Tom and Mary will help out, and I think it will do my mother good to get back to work.'

'Why don't we take Mrs Bishop with us?'

'No, she'll do better with Mary.'

A silence falls. He blows his nose again, and tucks the handkerchief back into his waistcoat pocket.

'When shall you call the banns?'

He gives me a curious look. 'When we return from Brighton.'

'So you have nothing more to say to me?' I know he

is unwell and grieving, but I had expected more, a little more openness, or vitality, or even a hint of ardour. I had foolishly hoped that my acceptance of his offer might indeed bring him a little comfort or cheer.

He looks at me properly for the first time since he has returned from the funeral. I expected him to look sad, but I didn't expect disappointment and confusion to show so easily on his face; I daresay it shows on mine too. For a man who has just become engaged – or I suppose he has, for he has not asked me and I have not agreed to it, as far as I remember – he seems remarkably unmoved.

He blows his nose.

The ever-surprising Harry Bishop says in a thoughtful voice, 'I think I'd like to go to bed now.'

16

Sophie

'Oh!' I try not to show how flustered I am or how aroused I am either at his sudden suggestion. What does it matter if he sneezes a few times beneath the sheets? 'Now? With your mother and all your relatives in the house?'

'Why should they mind? I didn't sleep at all last night and I'm unwell. They've all drunk so much I daresay they'll scarcely notice my absence at dinner.'

'*Your* absence?'

'Yes. If you could let them know, Sophie, I'd much appreciate it. I'll bid you goodnight, then.'

And he walks past me, pausing at the door of the kitchen to have a short conversation with the cook. I hear the words 'pick it up from the floor and wash it', and wonder which part of the dinner suffered a mishap. It seems dinner may prove as great a disappointment as

Harry's offer to make an honest woman of me. So I return to the parlour, where card games are underway. Mrs Bishop has offered the hotel as a stake, and I hope the ladies are too drunk to remember anything of it when the time comes to settle up.

Amelia, who is looking rather wobbly and pink-cheeked from the claret, clutches my sleeve when I enter the room. 'Is everything well?' she asks.

'Very well. I'm to come to Brighton with you tomorrow.'

'Oh, good. Mrs Marsden, you don't mind, do you?'

'Not at all. I am sure everything will go well with Lord Shad.'

'Oh.' She bites her lip. 'You think he will give his consent?'

'He may insist you wait a few years for you are very young.'

She nods, but to my surprise looks relieved. Possibly her short time with my father has disillusioned her about a career on the stage, and I am sorry that Amelia has lost her fire and passion so early. On the other hand, neither of us may have any idea what we are saying, for I am swilling the best claret to catch up with the other ladies, and Amelia's speech is very slightly slurred.

Dinner, a drunken, raucous affair, steadies but does not stop the claret consumption. At one point I find myself and Amelia standing on chairs, both of us swaying mightily, and singing, to the delight of the company. It is quite like old times.

My father, discovering Harry is absent, decides he shall take over as host, which he does with great energy and charm.

'But where is your young man?' he says at one point, when the two of us somehow find a quiet space while the celebrations rage around us.

'Asleep. He has caught my cold.'

'Aha. And is everything settled between you?'

'I believe so.'

'Sophie, my darling, surely you know. Did he propose marriage or not?'

He talked of marriage, it is true, although with a singular lack of passion. I was present, and so that must mean a proposal. 'He did, sir, and I have accepted him.'

'My child!' He looks around for his glass and I fear he is about to propose a toast.

'No, Papa, if you please. We wish to keep it quiet for the moment. Will you wait until we return from Brighton? It does not seem proper with his father just buried.'

'Of course, my petal. Of course. You are such a tender creature.' He gazes at me with brimming eyes. 'I want nothing more than your happiness. And don't worry about Sloven; I shall disallow the engagement. Besides, we're in too far for him to withdraw his financial support.'

I believe he may be sincere, or the wine makes him so and makes me receptive to his sentiments. Our fond embrace is cut short as Sylvia, skirts tucked up to facilitate the technique of tossing a bottle beneath her raised leg, juggles glasses and bottles to the delight of the audience.

Harry

The company is, in a word, crapulous the next morning, and the family parlour and the hotel dining room are littered with detritus from the merrymaking, including my nephew Richard fast asleep under the table among breadcrusts and bones. I believe all of the good claret may have been consumed and hope my father would have approved.

I set the staff to cleaning. Their confusion speaks not only of overindulgence the night before, but of neglect in the forgotten arts of sweeping and scrubbing. I offer dire threats if the hotel is not cleaned thoroughly by the time I return, and seek my mother who is still abed.

'What do you want at this time of day, Harry?' My mother pokes her head, crowned with an elaborate nightcap, from the covers.

'I've come to bid you farewell, Ma. I'm off to Brighton

with Miss Amelia and Mrs Marsden. We have to leave early for the morning coach.'

'Must you go?'

'I regret I must.' I speak as gently as I can but she cries anyway and clings to me.

'Don't stay too long, Harry. I need you here.'

'I know. It won't take me too long to conclude business with his lordship.'

'Well, he'll be glad to get his ward back, I should think. And how do things stand with you and dear Sophie?'

I consider before answering. 'We are on cordial terms.'

'Cordial terms! You're a catch, now, Harry, with the hotel yours. She'll have you, I warrant.' She nudges me. 'Come, you don't want your old mother working her fingers to the bone.'

'Oh, absolutely, Ma. My bride should work her fingers to the bone instead.'

'She may have some scandal in her past, but she's a sensible, clever girl, I think, and will do you proud.' She frowns. 'Mr Marsden asked me last night if I wished to invest in his theatrical company. What do you think, my dear? He is a most persuasive gentleman.'

Relief that my mother approves of my choice of a bride turns to anger. 'Absolutely not! I trust you made no sort of commitment. He's not to be trusted. Pray do not receive him before I return home. Besides, Pa left the books in such a state I don't even know how much money we have.'

'Very well.' She sighs. 'Go along with you, then, my dear. No, don't kiss me. I don't want to catch your cold. Do you have enough handkerchiefs with you?'

How is it that my mother can make me feel like a schoolboy? I go downstairs to the parlour where Sophie and Amelia, both of them pale and yawning, await me.

I bow to one and smile on the other, but they receive my greeting with very little interest. I offer them willow from my medicine chest and take a tincture of rosemary for my own ills, and we set off, with Richard driving. Rather, when I say Richard drives, he sits, a crumpled, unwell presence, on the driver's seat, and the horse promptly goes to sleep. I am compelled to take the reins myself – I believe the horse will find his own way home without Richard's participation – and so we make our way through the streets to the far better appointed and respectable inn, the White Horse Inn on Picadilly, where the Brighton coach stops. I find myself looking upon the appointments of the inn with a keen eye, noticing the cleanliness of the staff's linen and the efficiency with which horses are changed. Bishop's Hotel does not compare favourably with this establishment, but where it does exceed is in the cordiality of the staff (although I expect that today, following the excesses of the previous day, a general surliness will prevail).

We have inside seats, and both ladies compose themselves to sleep, gradually falling upon my shoulders so I am hard pressed to take my handkerchief from my pocket. I fall asleep myself, and dream of accounts and ledgers and bills, and the shock of coming upon quite ordinary items in the house that remind me of my father: his pipe, the china dog upon the parlour mantelpiece that he glued together after Joseph and I broke it as children, his hat hanging from a peg as though at any moment he would take it and strut into the yard as a carriage arrived.

I never knew I should miss him so.

I never anticipated how lonely I should feel without him.

We arrive in Brighton in the late afternoon. The passengers stir and stretch and there is a general air of excitement as the coach reaches the crest of the Downs and then begins the steep descent into town. Spread out before us are the baubles and bubbles of the Royal Pavilion, smoky huddles of the old town cheek by jowl with elegant new terraces for the fashionable, and beyond that the sea, blue and hazy and enticing, dotted with the sails of small craft, fishing vessels and yachts, and closer to shore, bathing machines. I pull the window open, despite protests from our fellow travellers, and the usual scents of a town, horses and coal-smoke and closely packed humanity, are accompanied by a faint whiff of salt.

Sophie gazes out of the window. I know she has been here before, doubtless on some gentleman's arm, his prized possession, and I wonder if that is the cause of the sadness on her face, but her expression changes and she claps her hands like a child, reaching for my arm.

'Look, Harry, the sea! Is it not a splendid sight?'

'I wish my father could have seen it.' And then I remember my mother telling him of how she would take him to the sea for his health as he lay dying and grope for my handkerchief.

Sophie says nothing; she does not need to, for her face expresses profound sympathy and understanding, and the touch of her hand on mine is far more eloquent than any words.

'I hope I don't catch your cold,' Amelia says, oblivious of what has passed between me and Sophie. 'I'm hungry.'

'You sound like . . .' Sophie hesitates, but continues '. . . like your nephews who want to eat all the time. Why, Amelia, you are an aunt! It makes you sound so very grown-up.'

'Oh. I suppose I am. An aunt, I mean. And now I am indeed grown-up.'

Sophie touches her wrist. 'My dear, if there is anything you wish to tell me . . .'

'No!' Amelia looks to me. 'Harry, when do we arrive?'

But at that moment the driver blows the horn and bellows that we have arrived in Brighton, and the coach turns from the bustle of the street into the courtyard of the Ship Hotel.

'Oh, Harry, Mrs Marsden, may we go to the sea?' Amelia is jumping up and down like a small child. Any nervousness she has concerning her reunion with the family has dissipated. She tips her head back to look at a seagull floating lazily overhead.

'Be careful of your complexion,' Sophie says, smiling at Amelia's excitement. To me, she says in a quiet voice, 'Do you think it appropriate that she addresses you as "Harry"? I shall mention it to her.'

We leave our luggage in the inn and venture on to the promenade where the fashionable saunter in bright sunlight. I shall have to find Sophie lodgings for the night, unless the family relents and allows her to stay. She looks quite at home here, strolling arm in arm with Amelia, although she is plainly dressed. You might think them a couple of upper servants on their half-day off.

I take a deep breath of sea air, invigorated and a little more cheerful. All will be well. Here, a day's journey from London, with the sea spread like a great shifting and glittering sheet of blue, my worries and sadness recede for a little, and I am glad of it.

Sophie and Amelia, meanwhile, still excited as a pair of children – even with her worldly and wicked experiences, Sophie still retains a childlike capacity for innocent pleasure – descend worn stone steps on to the pebbled beach. A fisherman, sitting on an upturned boat and mending his nets, gives their ankles a good inspection.

Hand in hand, the two women race to the edge of the water, where they jump and squeal as waves break, and Amelia plucks a piece of seaweed from the surf. I make my way over the stones to join them.

'It is wonderful!' Amelia says and then shrieks as the waves break over her feet.

'Come, we must go to the Earl of Beresford's house.' The sooner this business is over the better; and at this time of day, when the fashionable, having paraded up and down the sea front, retire to their houses, we are likely to find Lord Shad at home.

'I suppose so,' Amelia mutters, eyes downcast.

Of course she is afraid.

Sophie stands at the water's edge, her bonnet scandalously removed, her dark hair lifting and loosening in the wind. I am struck once again by the purity of her profile, her beauty, her expressions that change like the sea and the sky, revealing every thought and emotion.

I have made a terrible mistake.

Sophie

So far, so good. I thought I recognized a few members of the ton taking the air, but I am dressed so dowdily, and walking with two people who are not fashionable, that I might as well be invisible, a thought that cheers me. Once I would have been mightily insulted not to be recognized as a pretty, fashionable, and influential personage. The advantage is, of course, that now I may run on the beach and enjoy the waves and pebbles and sunlight.

That was not the behaviour of the scandalous Mrs Wallace, whose wickedness was far more polished and sophisticated. She would be perched on a phaeton with her latest lover, dressed at the height of fashion with a parasol protecting her from the ravages of the sun.

I am glad to see Harry is cheered somewhat, too. The strain has lifted a little from his face and he even smiles at Amelia as she gets her slippers wet in the surf and carefully places a handful of seaweed in her reticule. I am not sure what she intends to do with it, and I suspect it may draw flies or stink in a few days, but I will not spoil her pleasure. She has the wrath of Lord Shad to look forward to, poor child. He may be soft-hearted with his little children, but the question of his sister's honour may well rouse him to anger.

'Harry, do you think we can bathe?' Amelia says. 'And

ride on a donkey? I should so like to do that. And someone said they have assemblies at the Ship Inn. And I shall need a parasol and a wide-brimmed bonnet against the sun, and—'

'I'm afraid our visit can be only of a very short duration,' Harry says. 'We must return to London tomorrow.'

'Very well, Harry.' Amelia's words may seem acquiescent, but she sighs heavily and rolls her eyes.

Oh, Lord, he wants to drag me back to Bishop's Hotel so I can lawfully reside in a parish and the banns can be called. But does he really expect Lord Shad to allow his sister to return to London with us? I certainly cannot vouch for my father as a suitable person to protect her, nor his theatre as a place where Amelia may learn her trade.

Or, heavens, does he expect Lord Shad to cast Amelia out, which, sad to say, many a man in his position and with a wayward female relative, would do?

Amelia and I tidy ourselves as best we can in the brisk wind and we make our way back to the stone steps and up on to the promenade, and so to the house that the Earl of Beresford, the highest member of the Trelaise family, has taken for the summer. Harry, naturally, has the address.

It is a most impressive house and we linger outside, admiring the dark green of the railings and the pleasant beige stone of which the house is built. Stairs lead down to the servants' entrance, where someone, shovelling coal from the sound of it, whistles loudly.

Amelia seems to have lost what nerve she has. She clutches Harry's arm. 'I don't think I can!'

He pats her hand. 'I will look after you, never fear.'

I interrupt this scene, which smacks of impropriety to me. What if Lord Shad, looking out from a window, sees his half-sister, who is supposed to be in Bath, on such intimate terms with his house steward?

'I am damned if I will go into the servants' entrance,' I say. 'I'm no longer Lord Shad's servant and I shall not behave as such.'

Harry mutters something that sounds like '... and you never did,' but I ignore him and mount the steps to the front door. I grasp the bell handle and give it a good tug, aware that almost certainly the butler spies on us through a side window, assessing our birth, rank, fortune, and the cost of our clothes.

I wish we had not dabbled in the sea but it is too late.

The door swings open and an imposing butler, who I am sure believes he is the future heir to a dukedom, stands there. He says nothing but the eloquent lift of his eyebrows expresses dismay and profound sorrow that such a person should wish for admittance. The only thing that spoils his dignity is a handful of leashes, at the end of which prance a collection of small, yipping dogs, straining to leave the house.

A very familiar collection.

'Why,' I say in delight, 'is the Countess of Dachault here?'

Amelia bends to pat the dogs, who fawn over her, licking her hands and face. 'Oh, what lovely dogs! Are they yours, sir?'

The butler's face assumes an expression of horror and disgust as though Amelia has suggested he make pets of the rats in the cellar. 'They are not, miss. And yes, ma'am, the Countess of Dachault visits, and these belong to her.'

'Sophie!' Claire, Countess of Dachault, has apparently heard her name. She appears behind the butler. 'Sophie, what are you doing here? Yes, Hoskins, you may let the footman take the dogs outside and admit Mrs—' she stops herself just in time. 'That is, Mrs Marsden and her companions.'

'May I not go with the dogs?' Amelia says.

'No,' Harry and I say together.

'What are you doing here?' Claire mutters to me as she takes my arm and pulls me into the house. 'I thought you'd left the position. I was quite annoyed, Sophie. I thought you might have made the effort to last a little longer.'

'I'm sorry. I'll explain it later. But you seem very at home here.'

'I'm as thick as thieves with the Countess of

Beresford,' Claire says. 'Do you know her, Sophie?'

'No.' I regret I know the Earl, who pursued me for a time, given to pinning me into corners and breathing heavily. 'It's a little late for afternoon calls, is it not?'

'Oh, this is Brighton. Informality reigns. We are in and out of each other's houses all day long. Do come in. But who is this lovely young girl? Surely you're not Miss Trelaise? Shad has told us all about you.'

Amelia curtsies, to my relief making no attempt to deny the surname. 'How do you do, ma'am.'

'What charming manners! But aren't you supposed to be in Bath? And the, ah, gentleman?' Claire looks at Harry and then at me.

I introduce them without telling Claire he is Lord Shad's steward.

'Is he your lover?' she whispers, giggling. 'He's rather stern, isn't he?'

'He is in mourning, Claire. Have you no sense of propriety?'

'My, you are a reformed character.' She winks at me.

Beresford's house is of such palatial size that our whispered conversation has lasted the length of the hall, and footmen wearing suspiciously Oriental livery – well, we are in Brighton and a stone's throw from the Pavilion – open double doors to an opulent drawing room. Copper dragons writhe around lamps, silk hangings line the walls, and the Countess of Beresford, a beautiful fair-haired woman, entertains her female friends at tea and cards.

Charlotte rises to her feet and runs towards us. 'Amelia! What the devil are you doing here? My dear Sophie!' She captures me in a hearty embrace. 'I trust you have come to your senses and returned to employment with us. But why are you all here? And Harry! We were so sorry to hear about your father.'

'Is that the gentleman who delivered Harriet?' Claire whispers to me. 'Charlotte has done nothing but sing the praises of both of you since she arrived, and she thinks he is your lover, so I shall get to the truth.'

'Ma'am,' Harry says to Charlotte, 'I must speak with Lord Shad.'

Amelia, poor child, clutches my hand. 'Mrs Marsden, I can't do this.'

'Of course you can! Don't worry, I am sure your brother will forgive you.'

'It's not that,' she says. 'It's—'

But at that moment, Claire's pack of dogs burst into the drawing room, dragging a footman behind them.

'Sit!' says Harry, and they obediently drop to the carpet, gazing at him with adoring eyes.

'The gentlemen are out sailing. We expect them back at any time. Charlotte, did I mention to you that Sophie and I went to school together? Oh, the times we had. Come, let me introduce you to our hostess, the Countess of Beresford.' And she takes us across the room to meet Ann Trelaise, Countess of Beresford, who is even more haughtily aristocratic than her butler. Until, that is, Charlotte nudges her and whispers in her ear and they giggle together like a pair of schoolgirls.

And then I realize what is missing from this assembly: no children underfoot, not even little Harriet in Charlotte's arms.

Harry asks after the children's health, and we discover that Lord Shad has taken his nephew John sailing – Amelia looks at me in surprise to hear him described thus – and the little boys and Harriet are upstairs in the nursery. 'Indeed, yes, you are like a dairy cow,' the Countess of Beresford says in a cool yet affectionate voice to Lady Shad.

'And is your health returned, ma'am?' I ask Charlotte. 'You look very well.'

'Now she gets some sleep she gets on very well,' the Countess of Beresford says.

'I can speak for myself, Ann,' says Lady Shad. 'Yes, thank you, Sophie, the sea air has proved most pleasant.'

But at that moment male voices are heard, for the gentlemen have indeed returned, and they swagger into the drawing room, full of talk about nautical matters, some of them boasting fierce sunburns.

John sees Amelia first and breaks off from the group to greet her. 'What are you doing here? Did you know I am Lord Shad's nephew? Is not that a fine thing?'

'Yes, and I am your aunt,' Amelia replies, 'and I can tell you what to do, so pray do not be so full of yourself.'

Lord Shad joins us. 'Amelia, we understood you were in Bath.' And then, turning to Harry, 'My commiserations, sir, on your loss. But what is Amelia doing here with you? And Mrs Marsden?'

'I ran away,' Amelia says. 'I never went to Bath. I ran away to London. Harry and Mrs Marsden found me.'

'Come.' Shad takes her arm and leads us to the far end of the drawing room where we stand unnoticed by the rest of the company, who are regaled by unlikely tales of expert seamanship.

'What happened to you?' Lord Shad asks. His voice is gentle but a steely glint in his eyes does not bode well.

'I— I ran away, but I was fortunate enough to meet Mrs Marsden's father, who was very respectable and kind. He runs a theatre company and I—'

'What the devil possessed you, Amelia? To lie to your family, to risk yourself so?'

'Mrs Marsden said – I am sorry, sir, I am truly sorry – that I could make a living upon the stage.'

'What!' Lord Shad turns to me now and I doubt whether I have ever seen anyone so angry.

'Why, Sophie!'

I turn at the familiar voice. *Oh, no.*

'Oh. Charlie. Oh, fancy seeing you here.' This must

be a bad dream. Charlie Fordham, my former protector, whom I last saw the day I met Harry Bishop; the day our establishment was dismantled and Charlie was banished to the country.

Charlie, as handsome as ever, hair and skin burnished by the sun, takes my hand and kisses it. 'I came into my majority last week, Sophie, and I was wondering if—'

'Charlie, we are having a private discussion,' Lord Shad says. 'If you please—'

'Lovely Sophie Wallace,' Charlie says, kissing my other hand and gazing at me. 'How I've missed you.'

'Who?' Lord Shad looks at him and then at me. 'You are the notorious Mrs Sophie Wallace?'

'I can explain,' I say. 'Charlie, please go away. You are making things worse.'

'You're ruined,' Lord Shad says to Amelia. 'You, Mrs Wallace, pray leave this house, and you, Mr Bishop, did you contrive to ruin my family by introducing her into our midst?'

'No, she's not. She's Sophie Marsden,' Amelia says in confusion. 'She has always been very respectable and very kind to me, and Mr Bishop also. They came to London to find me at great inconvenience to themselves. And I know I'm ruined, sir, because I met Mrs Henney as I left the village and I told her I was going to London to be an actress.'

'Oh good God,' Lord Shad says. 'Could this be any

worse? Do you seek to disgrace my— your family entirely? What the devil am I to do?'

'You need have no concern about Miss Amelia's reputation,' Harry Bishop says. 'She and I have an understanding and I wish to ask permission to marry her.'

Sophie

My legs feel as though they will not support me and I sit down on the nearest sofa, a bright green thing with a back carved in the shape of a dragon and exceedingly uncomfortable.

Lord Shad's voice is a quiet, menacing whisper which I am sure the entire drawing room can hear. 'You proposed marriage to my sister?'

'But I did not agree to marry you, Harry!' Amelia says.

'What!' Harry says.

'I said you must talk to Lord Shad,' Amelia says. 'I didn't say I would marry you. I didn't say I wouldn't either. I was upset.'

Harry blinks at her. 'But— but of course I must talk to Lord Shad. It is only proper. You have not reached your majority—'

'She is seventeen,' Lord Shad says. 'What were you

thinking, Bishop? Are you so ambitious that you would marry into my family? You expected a dowry with her hand?'

'My lord, your sister is ruined. You have said it yourself. I was afraid you would cast her off, and then what would become of her? Besides, I need someone to help me run the hotel, a woman who is not afraid of hard work.' Harry, suddenly, looks murderously angry himself. 'You impugn my honour, sir. I certainly did not expect anything from you or your family.'

'Shad, you are not to call him out!' Lady Shad plants herself firmly between the two men.

'But I don't want to marry him!' Amelia cries. 'I like you well enough, Harry, and I am most grateful that you and Mrs Marsden came to rescue me, even though I didn't want to be rescued. And I don't want to run a hotel. Sir,' appealing to Lord Shad, 'please do not make me marry him.' She sniffs. 'I did not think it polite to refuse him outright.'

Finally I find my voice. 'But— but you proposed to me, Harry!'

'I beg your pardon, ma'am. I did propose to you, shortly before we left Lord Shad's house, and you turned me down.'

'No, not then. In your office at the hotel.'

'But— but that was when I told you I was engaged to Amelia.'

'You did not! You talked of marriage and I— I agreed.' But I remember how indirect he was, how he never actually asked me. I remember with a pang his lack of affection, his sorrow. And his behaviour, his increased familiarity with Amelia – everything falls into place and makes sense. Harry is to marry Amelia.

I have lost him.

'I thought I told you to leave this house, ma'am,' Lord Shad interjects.

'It is not your house, sir, and I have not yet spoken—'

'Sophie, dear, do not argue with Shad. It does no good when he is angry.' Lady Shad takes my arm and glares at Harry. 'What the devil are you about, Harry? Playing fast and loose with Sophie and Amelia? I had not expected it of you, and particularly when it was so obvious that you are head over heels in love with Sophie!'

'Head over heels?' Harry says.

'So obvious?' I say at the same time.

'Yes, indeed.' Lady Shad turns to her husband. 'My dear, did you not realize who Sophie was?'

'I did not, ma'am, and if I had I should never have entrusted any member of my family to her influence, you included, Charlotte.' He looks as though he would like to murder someone, and I am not sure which of us he will choose.

Our conversation, conducted at the far end of the salon, and in whispers to avoid the intervention of other guests in the house, nevertheless attracts some attention. Charlie lurks around nearby, gazing at me with the sort of expression I am all too familiar with, doubtless wondering where the nearest bedchamber is and how soon he can get me into it.

'Charlie, dear,' Lady Shad says, 'pray go and join the others. Now, as for my guessing your identity, dear Sophie, I did so some time ago, for I am very fond of the gossip papers. I can only take it as a great compliment that you, Shad, never looked at another woman in London and so did not know who she was. Harry, it seems you acted with the utmost gallantry in offering to restore Amelia's reputation through marriage.'

'Gallantry!' Lord Shad echoes. 'Some would call it that, and others, idiocy, to become engaged to two women at once.'

'He's certainly not engaged to me.' Amelia blows her nose. 'I think I have caught the cold. I'm so sorry, Sophie, about Harry's proposal of marriage. I should have refused him outright. But then I did ask you if you minded that I might marry him, and you said you did not.'

I think back to that short, drunken exchange when she asked me if I thought Lord Shad would give his consent to— to something, and I had not even thought of matrimony. 'I thought you meant you wanted to ask Lord Shad's permission to remain in London and go on the stage.'

'Which you most certainly do not have!' Lord Shad said. 'It's you and the poultry, miss, for the next ten years, and the only place you'll go to outside the house is church.' He looks upon her with a little more kindness. 'We'll weather out the scandal, my dear. Tongues will wag for a time and then it will be forgotten.' He turns to me. 'You, however, Mrs Wallace, I cannot forgive. You led this child astray, you came to my house under false pretences, and with the collusion of my house steward—'

'I blackmailed him.'

'Oh, nonsense,' Lady Shad says. 'Harry would not let himself be blackmailed. And Shad, one thing your family has in common is that you are all like horses with blinkers. Amelia is no better or worse; she is dead set upon going on the stage and will make our lives a misery if you deny her.'

'I certainly don't intend, ma'am, to have my sister—'

But Lady Shad interrupts him. 'And this is *Sophie*, Shad. Sophie who sings so prettily and who played with our children and is a paragon of genteel behaviour. She came with the recommendation of the Countess of Dachault, a most respectable lady, who certainly knew of her past. I suggest you practise a little Christian forgiveness, sir. Besides,' and her voice takes on a silky sweetness, 'I believe you have done your share of running after actresses in your time. Let him who is without sin cast the first stone.'

'You forget your place, ma'am,' Lord Shad says.

'On the contrary, I do not. Come, Sophie, you and Harry must take a walk together and get this sorry business sorted out. And Harry, after that you must go to our house and collect your things, and Shad will give you a very good wedding gift.'

A growl of disapproval erupts from his lordship.

Harry offers me his arm and we make our bow and curtsy to the assembled company and leave the house.

Harry

I have been a fool. When I saw Sophie's stricken face I knew what I had done and I knew I must persuade her that although I have been both an idiot and a poltroon, I shall be so no longer.

As though we have arranged to walk that way, we retrace our footsteps and descend once more on to the beach, where the only sound is that of breaking waves and the crunch and slide of stones beneath our feet.

Her face is turned away, hidden by her bonnet. 'You proposed to Amelia. When?'

'When I escorted her back to her lodgings. At the time it seemed the right thing to do.'

'So you turned to the nearest woman. I suppose it

makes very little difference which one, merely that she is not too proud to be proprietress of Bishop's Hotel.'

I wish I could see her face, now further obscured by a floating lock of dark hair tugged free by the wind. We are alone on the beach, for the fishermen have gone, leaving their boats dragged up high above the tideline. 'I love you, Sophie. Tell me you are not indifferent to me.'

She shrugs and bends to pick something from the stones, a piece of glass now rounded and frosted by the pressure of waves and sand to a delicate green opacity. 'Maybe it's too late, Harry. But, why? Why did you propose to Amelia?' Her voice quivers and I realize how deeply I have injured her.

I remove my glasses, specked with sea foam, and polish them on my cuff. 'I am sorry, Sophie. I felt it was my fault. All of it. If I had not allowed you to stay in the house, then she would not have been inspired to go upon the stage or run away to London.'

'Oh nonsense.' She turns to face me, and if her eyes are wet maybe it is because the wind is so sharp. 'You heard what Lady Shad said – the whole family is wilful and do what they wish with no thought of consequences. Amelia dreamed of the stage long before she met me. You read that page in her diary. That you wished to make amends is admirable, but it was not your fault. Harry, you suffered a severe loss; did you not consider your judgement to be impaired? Do you think proposal to any woman, under the circumstances, would have been wise?'

'My judgement has been impaired ever since meeting you.'

'A compliment?' She smiles a little.

I take a deep breath. 'Maybe you are right. But the hotel . . .'

'You'll manage. Your mother will rally. There's no need to rush into anything, particularly matrimony.'

She's right. We walk along the shore and she takes my arm as though it is the most natural thing in the world, and I consider how odd it is that we have come to this understanding, this peaceful place, now we both know marriage is out of the question. Or is it?

'Sophie, when I proposed – or you thought I did so, and I am most sorry that I did not trust you enough to confide in your properly – did you really want to marry me?'

'I don't know. You lacked a certain passion, but that was understandable.' She sighs. 'I regret to say I accepted – or I thought I did so – because I felt sorry for you, and I do like your family so very much. But then you proposed to me the time before because Lord Shad had told you to do so, which is an equally dreadful reason to consider marriage.' She giggles. 'I was much surprised when you invited me to bed.'

'I did *what*?' This I don't remember at all, and I

regret my first reaction is furious disappointment that I missed the opportunity.

'Well.' She laughs a little and squeezes my arm. 'You spoke to me of marriage and then expressed an interest in going to bed. Naturally I thought the two were related, but you were feeling unwell, it turned out. The wonder of it is that I did not make an absolute fool of myself.'

'I was the one who played the fool.'

She slides her hand down my arm and we stand, hands clasped. 'No, you were never a fool, Harry.'

'What shall we do, Sophie?'

'Oh, I suppose I'll go back to London and to my father's theatre and darn his stockings since Amelia is no longer available.' She smiles. 'I shall be very near Bishop's Hotel, Harry. I hope I shall call on your mother to take tea often.'

'She'll like that. I intend to improve the hotel immensely. I've often thought it would be a good place for society to stop for refreshment before making their grand entrance into the fashionable part of town.'

'Why, that's an excellent idea!' She beams with delight.

'Sophie, may I ask what you intend to do about Jake Sloven?'

'I can handle him. He's a soft fool and he'll do anything I tell him to.'

'And Charlie Fordham?'

'Oh, Charlie,' she says with a rueful smile. 'I don't think I need to worry about Charlie Fordham, and you certainly should not. I am a free woman. I think I'll go back to the Ship Inn, now, Harry.'

'May— may I call upon you in London?' I feel ridiculously shy and, from the pinkness that steals over her face, I suspect she feels the same.

'Of course. I should be most disappointed if you do not, although I assure you I shall throw myself in your way as much as possible on the pretext of calling on your mother.'

'So I may yet hope . . .' Her lips are close to mine, that wayward lock of hair blowing onto my cheek and binding me to her.

'Sophie!' It's a female voice and I turn to see a tall angular woman striding over the beach towards us, followed by one of Beresford's footmen.

'Oh, Lord,' mutters Sophie. She waves and calls out, 'Lizzie!' To me she says, 'She is Claire's secretary, Mrs Buglegloss. She was at school with us, too. She was always the well-behaved one.'

The woman approaches and looks upon our clasped hands with disapproval. The footman, puffing behind her, makes a grab at his wig as the sea breeze snatches it from his head, but it flies over the waves. We all watch as it lands on the water, where it floats briefly, tossed from side to side, and is investigated by a seagull.

'Oh, bugger,' mutters the footman, watching his wig sink to its watery grave and the seagull fly away. 'Old Hoskins'll fine me for sure.'

'Lizzie, this is Mr Bishop, who—'

'Yes, yes, I know. You must come back to the house immediately.' Mrs Buglegloss is highly agitated and out of breath.

Sophie smiles agreeably. 'Oh, I don't think so.'

'Sophie, I must insist!'

'You're almost as bossy as Claire these days,' Sophie says. 'Very well. I suppose you will not tell me what has happened? Are Lady Shad's children well?'

'Oh, yes. Yes.' Lizzie grabs Sophie's other hand. 'Hurry!'

'Stop pulling me about, you great beanstalk. Your legs are twice the length of mine.'

'There is no need for indelicacy!' Mrs Buglegloss snaps. 'And the next time we recommend you for a position – if we ever do, which is most unlikely – I trust you'll not create such chaos in the household you serve.'

'I? I create chaos? Oh no, you are mistaken. Did you not hear Lady Shad say I was a model of propriety?'

'Stop teasing, Sophie,' I say. 'Mrs Buglegloss, pray calm yourself. We do not want either of you ladies to twist an ankle on these stones. Let us walk on the parade.'

Sophie looks at the sea with some reluctance, and

then at me with a smile. Within a few minutes we find ourselves back at the Earl of Beresford's house. The upstairs windows glow with candlelight, for the company now dresses for dinner.

Hoskins, the butler, opens the front door to us. The door to the kitchen downstairs is open and I can hear the familiar mix of cursing and the clatter of pans that mean dinner is almost ready.

Hoskins inspects us and finds us wanting, for we are windswept and untidy, but allows the footman to escort Sophie and me to a small room at the rear of the house; Mrs Buglegloss, shaking her head, disappears upstairs.

The scatter of feminine items in the room – an embroidery frame, some magazines – indicate this is the preserve of the ladies of the house, a private parlour. But the company in the room is masculine – a tall, fair-haired gentleman who introduces himself as the Earl of Beresford, Lord Shad, and another gentleman.

The Earl rubs his hands with some glee, as though anticipating a delightful treat, but Lord Shad looks exceedingly grave. And the third gentleman, smart in regimentals, strolls towards us, pausing to toss his cigar into the fireplace.

'My dear girl!' he exclaims.

The room is very quiet as though none of us dares breathe. The fire snaps and crackles.

'Do you know this gentleman, Sophie?' Lord Shad asks.

'Yes.' She sways. 'Yes, I do. What the devil are you doing here, Rupert?'

And before I can reach her she falls on to the floor in a dead faint.

18

Harry

'Fetch her some brandy!' I shout to the nearest person, who happens to be the Earl of Beresford. He looks around helplessly as though he does not know where the brandy is kept in his house.

I kneel by her and for one dreadful moment think she is dead, she is so pale and still, and loosen her bonnet strings. 'Sophie!'

Her eyelids flutter and she gives a strange little gasp, her lips moving as though she is trying to tell me something. I remember with horror my mother's account of my father's fatal swoon.

I raise her in my arms and Lord Shad, who has acquired a glass of brandy, tips some into her mouth. She splutters, coughs, and comes back to life, and I help her to the sofa. The regimental gentleman, meanwhile, stands looking on without a word, and the Earl flaps his hands in a helpless sort of way. 'Shall I send for a woman?' he asks.

'What on earth for?' I return. 'Who the devil are you?' I ask the other gentleman.

'Captain Rupert Wallace, at your service, sir.'

I doubt he's at my service at all, and acknowledge him with a nod of my head. Her husband! She had told me she was widowed.

'You look quite splendid, my dear, if a little green around the gills,' the Captain says to Sophie. 'I've been meaning to have a happy reunion with you for some time, but when I get to London, what do I find? The fascinating Mrs Wallace has disappeared entirely, which is a bit of an embarrassment for me, my dear. For I'd heard you were living in high style, and I'm afraid I have run up some shocking debts.'

'I thought you were dead,' she says. 'I read it in the newspaper. You were killed in Spain somewhere.'

'A great exaggeration.'

'I believe you abandoned this lady, your wife,' Lord Shad says. 'Pray drink the rest of the brandy, Sophie, it will do you good.'

'No. I'll get drunk. I suppose you want my money, Rupert?'

'*Our* money,' he says. 'What's yours is mine, my love. I heard dear old Lord Radding was very generous, and others, too.'

'You'd best go. You can't suddenly appear after ten years and make demands of me.'

'I can, my dear. The law says it is a husband's right.' He smirks and I become enraged at him for his his arrogance and swagger, the insolence with which he speaks to Sophie – *my* Sophie. Or so I thought, but all along she has been his.

'And I, sir, say you cannot.' My fists clench of their own accord.

'Who the devil are you?' he says. 'I see you've gone down in the world, Sophie, if this gentleman is your protector. What are you, sir, some sort of tradesman?'

I hit him. I haven't hit anyone in years, not since Joseph and I were boys together, and certainly I never hit Joseph with such angry violence. My knuckles connect painfully with his nose and he staggers and falls back, landing with little dignity on his arse. His face, now covered with blood, bears an expression of great surprise.

'Steady.' Lord Shad grips my arm, preventing me from launching myself upon Captain Wallace and doing further damage to him.

'Oh do stop it,' Sophie says.

Wallace rises to his feet and dabs at his nose with a handkerchief. 'Send me your friend, sir. I lodge at the Black Dog.'

He leaves with outraged dignity.

'Congratulations,' Lord Shad says. 'You've been raised to the level of a gentleman, Bishop.'

'What do you mean, sir?'

'He's challenged you to a duel. May I do the honours?'

I gape at him.

'Shad's offering to be your second, Harry,' Sophie says.

'Of course,' I say, dumbfounded. 'Thank you, my lord.'

He claps me on the shoulder. 'Call me Shad. I'm no longer your employer.'

'You have an excellent arm, Bishop,' the Earl of Beresford comments. 'I've rarely seen an amateur with such speed and force.'

'I suppose it's years of carrying trays, my lord. You build up strong muscles in your back and shoulders.' I feel dazed and lost, as I did when my father died; one part of me talks trivialities with very little effort, while the rest of me struggles to make sense of everything. A duel? It seems trivial and ridiculous.

'You and Sophie must talk,' Lord Shad says. 'Come, Beresford, we should go into dinner.'

Sophie and I are left alone in the room.

'You seem to have a certain affinity with deceased gentlemen. First Sloven and now a husband, miraculously returned from the dead.'

'It is unlike you to be unkind,' she says.

She looks defeated and unhappy, her usual spirits subdued, and no wonder. She says, 'I was very young. I thought I was in love. He went abroad to fight and I believed him dead, Harry. And now he'll kill you.'

'I may kill him.'

She shrugs. 'Maybe. He's a crack shot and he was a soldier. He'd never have let you hit him if you had not caught him unawares.'

'What do you mean? That I should have asked his permission to hit him?' I pace around the room; I'm in a devil of a mess now, in love with a woman married to someone else, facing my imminent demise at the hands of a jealous husband – or, if not a jealous husband, a greedy and unscrupulous one. 'What does he want from you, Sophie?'

'I have some money put away, in investments, and some property,' she says in a quiet voice. 'Doubtless he found out. I never told you of this, Harry, because it is my surety, my protection against a time when I should retire. Yet my wealth – such as it is – is not easily realized into cash, you understand, although he would insist I do so, and then squander it. Do you remember when I showed you Radding's will? I showed you only the paragraph relating to the bed. The rest was folded under so you could not read it, for I trust no one with that information. You can be assured that any woman of middling means and low birth will find herself plagued by men intending to relieve her of what wealth she possesses. I can tell you now because . . .'

'Because it's too late.'

She looks at me, startled. 'If that is what you wish to think.'

I shake my head, wondering that in the space of an hour I can have experienced bliss at the anticipation of a respectable, tender courtship and marriage, and now, absolute despair: the loss of the woman I love and my imminent demise at the hands of a murderous husband. My mind flies around as I think of making a will and writing my farewell letters (my poor mother!).

She stands. 'I may have been a fool at fifteen to elope with that man, but I assure you I have not been one since, not for any man.'

And she goes out of the room, leaving me dumbfounded.

I follow her, but she is nowhere to be seen. One of the footmen, obviously sent to wait for me, invites me downstairs to dine with the upper staff, which I do. I am not yet so much a gentleman that I consider it beneath my dignity, and I learn that Mrs Wallace dines upstairs.

Sophie

I am so angry, so hurt, that you might think I can only peck at my food. Indeed, it is not so. I eat to the extent that Lady Shad – or rather, Charlotte, for we are now on Christian name terms – asks me, sotto voce, whether there is a reason for my appetite, with a telling glance at my midriff.

'No, ma'am,' I say, mouth full. I certainly don't want to tell her of the existence of Captain Wallace; Shad will tell her soon enough. 'I am feeding a cold.'

'What on earth is going on, Sophie?' She stares as I help myself to a large slice of roast beef dripping gravy. 'Is your appetite the result of a broken heart? I take it that you and Harry have not come to an understanding?'

'Oh, I have come to a very good understanding of that gentleman.' I dab at the bodice of my dress where an overloaded forkful of food broke free and tumbled down my front. 'Do you think this will wash?'

'Well enough, I should think. I'll ask Ann's maid.'

'Thank you. I wish to ask Lord Shad something after dinner. I'm only warning you so that even if everyone assumes I'm flirting with him, you will know the truth.'

'Of course, but . . .' She shakes her head.

Across the table Charlie Fordham gazes at me.

'Charlie,' I say quietly to him in my most seductively thrilling tones. 'Oh, Charlie, dear . . .'

'Mrs Wallace?' He quivers with expectation like a terrier at a rat hole.

'Oh, Charlie, I should so like you to . . .'

'Yes, Mrs Wallace?'

'Help me to a dumpling, if you will.'

Charlotte and Claire giggle, Claire with her napkin actually stuffed into her mouth.

Charlie grins with great good nature and ladles a dumpling on to my plate. 'And is there any other way I may be of service to you, Mrs Wallace? Some more cabbage, perhaps?'

Our hostess the Countess of Beresford gazes at us with mild, aristocratic distaste from the end of the table.

'Oh, her,' Charlotte whispers with a regrettable lack of grammar. 'Sophie, you should hear her belch. Beresford taught her how to when it rained for a week in the country and they could not hunt.'

I take a mouthful of the dumpling and allow a footman to take my plate as the next cover is brought in.

'What's this, eh?' Dachault says, breaking off an interminable conversation with one of the other gentlemen on the subject of dogs. In front of him is a masterpiece of the pastry chef's creation, a towering concoction of cream and spun sugar studded with almonds, raspberries tumbling down its side.

'It's French. It's a Charlotte Russe,' the Countess of Beresford says, 'in honour of my dear friend.'

'A harlot something or other, did you say? Good lord. Well.' His lordship glances at his wife and her female friends, myself included, who laugh helplessly. 'Those Frenchies . . . did you ever run into such a thing, Shad?'

'Not on board ship. These, however . . .' Shad stares entranced at a pair of blancmanges, palest pink, each topped with a ripe strawberry. 'I've seen something like this before.'

'They are very fashionable!' the Countess of Beresford says, a spot of pink appearing on each cheek.

'Yes, but they look just like . . .' Amelia relapses into giggles as we all hush her.

'I'm sure every household has at least one pair like that,' Charlotte says. 'What do you think, Fordham?'

Dachault cuts into the Charlotte Russe and the blancmanges wobble in a most lifelike way.

The Countess of Beresford frowns as her guests burst into laughter and rises. 'Ladies,' she announces. 'Let us leave the gentlemen to their entertainment.'

She leads the way to the drawing room. As we leave, Charlotte leans to whisper something in her husband's ear, and he nods, and murmuring an excuse to the other men, accompanies us out of the drawing room.

'What may I do for you, Mrs Wallace?'

'Sir—' My voice catches in my throat. 'I beg your

pardon, I believe this cold lingers still. Will you ask a footman to accompany me this evening? I must go out for a little while.'

'Why, ma'am? Do you wish to interfere in a matter of honour between gentlemen?'

'Of course.'

'Very well, ma'am. It is most improper for you to call upon him.'

'I don't see why. I am married to him, after all; did he not say so?'

'He did.' He looks at me, assessing me. There's something of the rogue about this man, and I'm halfway to blurting out the truth to him. 'I should warn you that you may not be the only one calling upon Wallace tonight.'

'You will be there, sir?'

'Not I. As Bishop's second, I must advise him, when I see him later, to let the gentleman stew, but I doubt he'll take my advice. For all Captain Wallace's military prowess I should not be surprised if he quietly leaves town. His sort does not want trouble. I'll ask Beresford to send a footman with you.'

'And another thing, sir. If you were agreeable to it, I believe I could help Amelia get a real role on the stage. I am willing to become a patron of a theatre – not the one where my father currently directs, for they are not licensed for plays, only pantomime. And as a patron I can have influence over the choice of play and the casting.'

'That's most generous of you, ma'am. But all in good time. She acted foolishly and she'll cool her heels with the chickens for a while. It will do her good.' He smiles and bows.

Later that evening, accompanied by a footman, I leave the elegance of the new part of the town and make my way into the crooked, old streets where the over-hanging houses block what light there is from the stars and moon. We tread carefully to avoid the stinking gutters that run down the centre of each street. The footman is armed with a large cudgel, and figures who emerge from the shadows retreat as they see his threatening appearance.

'You're not going in there alone, ma'am,' he says when we reach the Black Dog. 'His lordship's orders.'

'Wait for me, if you please.' I hand him a sixpence, and he grins at the prospect of the Black Dog's refreshments. Since Shad has almost certainly tipped him too I wonder what sort of protection he will provide on the journey back.

I ask the surly fellow in the taproom for Captain Wallace and am led upstairs. Doubtless he has instructed any pretty woman to be sent to his chambers with no need for any questions, or else he expects me to arrive and beg him not to murder my lover. The staircase is creaking and narrow and a rat ambles across the landing, too fat and complacent to be disturbed by the arrival of myself and the boy who leads me.

'This 'un, miss,' the boy says, hand out, palm up. I hand over a penny and he clatters back downstairs.

I knock on the door and a grunt bids me enter.

Rupert Wallace sits, the remains of dinner on the table, a glass of wine in his hand. I suspect Shad is right in thinking that he plans to leave, for a portmanteau, lid open, and almost full, stands on the floor next to the bed.

'Why, Sophie, my dear. Have you come to share the connubial bed once more? How charming.' He rises to his feet, bows, and offers me a chair. Well, he never lacked manners.

'You always were an optimist, Rupert.' I take the chair and accept a glass of wine, which to my surprise is quite good. I am also not surprised that he keeps a second glass in the room, for doubtless he has been up to his usual tricks, cheating at cards and so on.

'So you've come to beg me to spare the life of your lover? What is he, a clerk?'

'Oh yes, the clerk who gave you that swollen nose. He's quite prepared to fight you, whereas I see you intend to leave.'

'Merely taking some better lodgings, my dear, which with your help I'll be able to afford. I'm most embarrassed to receive you in such poor surroundings.'

I smile and look at him over the rim of the wine glass.

'You've done quite well for yourself, haven't you, Sophie?'

'I have been fortunate, yes. Where have you been, Rupert?'

'Oh, abroad. Resigned my commission, spent some time in Dublin . . . I have family in Ireland, you know.'

I didn't know. He told me very little of himself and I'm not sure I can believe anything he says now. For all I know he could have been in London, swallowed up in the maw of that great city with all the other tricksters and rogues and rascals, spying upon me, collecting information, biding his time.

He takes my hand and kisses it. 'I've missed you, Sophie. I'm not saying I've lived like a monk, because it wouldn't be true, and you . . . well, enough said there. But we rubbed along together pretty well, didn't we?'

'I wish I could believe you. I was so very young. I'm different now.'

'You are. More beautiful, more assured. A woman, not a girl.' Fine words that, had he not gazed at my bosom with such interest, might have caused my heart to flutter a little, for once indeed I was desperately in love with him.

'I was so very naïve then. And you went away and I received but a handful of letters from you.' I take the small packet of papers, tied in pink ribbon, from my reticule.

'But, damnation, I wrote to you, Sophie. I swear I did. You must think me the greatest scoundrel,' he cries.

I let a long silence fall. Of course he is a great scoundrel; we both know it, as we both know that he never wrote to me once. And he seems to recollect this, and makes a great business of trimming and lighting a cigar at the candle upon the table, finally blowing out a fragrant cloud of smoke.

'What do you want, Sophie?' his voice has changed, become lower and more seductive, as he tries to take back the direction of our conversation. He glances at the packet of letters that lies beneath my hand on the table.

'I was so very foolish when I was fifteen,' I say.

'But so very lovely.'

'I knew little of the world or of men,' I say; not absolutely true, given my upbringing in the theatre and the series of substitute Mamas that populated my father's lodgings. 'And at boarding school . . .'

'That school,' he says, laughing. 'I remember the stories you told me of it. Trust your papa to choose such a worthless establishment.'

'He thought it would make me into a lady, but indeed, my education was sorely lacking. However, Rupert,' I lean forward and gaze into his eyes. 'Even I, with my schoolgirl deficiency in the study of the globes, knew that Scotland was more than one day's drive from

Shrewsbury and that the inhabitants of Gretna Green did not speak Welsh.'

A silence. A coal falls in the fireplace and the flame of the candle shivers as Rupert almost drops, and then steadies, his glass on the table.

'Clever little Sophie,' he says finally. He glances again at the packet of letters. 'But the world knows you as Mrs Wallace, and indeed, you've done pretty well with my name, have you not? So, how about a loan, my dear?'

I shake my head. 'I don't believe so. You see, I'd expect to be repaid.'

He stands and strolls to the fireplace. 'A little gift, then. I daresay your besotted little clerk knows about your past as Mrs Wallace, but for the right amount of money, I'll tell him our marriage was not legal. Coming from you, I doubt he'd believe it.'

'Oh, Rupert,' I say in the same tone of voice as when I asked Charlie for a dumpling earlier that evening, 'that is so very tempting. But I don't need your word for it. You see, after you went abroad, I met a certain Mr Bright, who much admired my performance on the stage. Imagine my surprise, for I had known him as the Reverend Mr Buckle who had officiated at our marriage. So,' holding up the packet of letters, 'I persuaded the gentleman to write his account of the matter.'

'Damn you!' George shouts and snatches the letters from me, tossing them on to the fire. He pokes them into a fierce blaze. 'Now what, Sophie?'

'Oh, those were laundry lists from the Earl of Beresford's house. Bright's statement is safely stored in my lawyer's office in London.'

Rupert lets his breath out in a long huff, and collapses back into his chair. He frowns and then bursts into laughter, and I'm reminded of what attracted me to him in the first place (other than the dash and glamour of a gentleman in regimentals looking upon me approvingly at church while the other pupils from Miss Lewisham's school giggled and nudged me in the ribs).

'Sophie, Sophie. I'm not a clever fellow, you know.' He pours me some more wine and takes another puff of his cigar. 'Not as clever as you. But now, this Mr Bishop. What is he? I need to know he'll treat you well, for I do care about you still – yes, you may smile and shake your head, but I was very happy with you. And the false marriage was a foolish thing, but you were a respectable pupil at Miss Lewisham's school, and I burned for you, Sophie. I thought it was the only way to ... well, you know. So tell me about Bishop.'

'He's a most respectable gentleman. He owns Bishop's Hotel.'

'Bishop's Hotel, eh? I stayed there a few times. How extraordinary. So, a man of property.'

And I realize my mistake.

He stubs out his cigar and leans forward, taking my hand. 'Consider this, then, Sophie, my love. The world knows you as Mrs Wallace and you've obviously committed adultery a few times. He won't want a scandal. He'll pay. It's a shabby enough place but in the right hands could be worth a mint. We make a good team, you and I. What do you say?'

The door to the bedchamber creaks open. Harry says, 'Yes, Mrs Wallace, what do you say?'

I don't know how long Harry has stood there, or what he has heard, but the conclusion he has reached is inevitable.

'Come in, my dear fellow,' Rupert cries. 'My lovely wife and I have a little business proposition to put to you.'

'I think not, sir.' Harry gives a stiff little bow, half insult, half formality. 'You may go to the devil, Wallace, and you too, Mrs Wallace. I trust I will see neither of you again.'

'Harry!' I cry, but he has gone.

'What about the duel?' Wallace shouts.

Harry shouts back that the Captain may do something anatomically impossible, even on a metaphorical level, regarding the duel, as he descends the stairs.

'Your apology is accepted,' Wallace bellows back. 'Whew. I thought he would have killed me,' says my gallant soldier lover. 'Well, Sophie, my dear, it looks like it is all over with him. You have nothing to lose now. What say you to throwing your lot in with me?'

Harry

'I beg your pardon, but this seems most unlike her.'
Shad pours me another glass of brandy. We are well on our way to getting drunk.

'I heard her say it with my own ears. With her own lips. You know what I mean.'

'You heard a few seconds of a conversation. You didn't hear her reply.'

'I didn't need to.' I gaze at the two brandy glasses in front of me, sliding in and out of each other, trying to decide which one to grasp. 'Perfidious Eve.'

'She was undressed? Well, that would be damning proof indeed.'

'No, sir! He was holding her hand, though.'

'Dear, dear,' says Shad. 'What depravity. Next you will tell me she was unchaperoned.'

'It is not a laughing matter, sir!'

'Sit down, sit down. I know. My apologies.' He pats

my arm. 'Now, what to do next. You still have some belongings at my house, I think.'

'I do, sir, but before I go there I should make sure all is well with the hotel.'

'An excellent idea.' I don't know why he seems so enthusiastic about my return to London, but then I don't seem to have much grasp of reality. 'And if you would, I have a few business matters I should like seen to. I need a new house steward, or at least a butler, and a nurse-maid. If you could interview some suitable applicants at one of the servant agencies, or possibly you know of some people – it should not take too long – I would be most grateful. But what of the duel?'

'I spoke to him in somewhat obscene terms of the duel and he seemed to think it was an apology. I wonder why I wanted to become a gentleman; you all seem to behave in a most peculiar way.'

'Charlotte and I and the children will miss you exceedingly,' he says. 'I'll stay at Bishop's Hotel when I come to attend sessions at the House. I've never much liked the family house and I rattle around in it alone. But Bishop, pray tell me what the state of the renovations was when you left the country.'

'Most excellent. Bricks and dust all over the floor and one of Bulmersh's men crushed his thumb. I helped them knock the hole in the wall. But, sir, where is Sophie now?'

He looks grave. 'I regret I cannot tell you that.'

Sophie

'I don't even like brandy.' Charlotte and I are busy getting drunk in her bedchamber. 'What shall become of me?'

'Oh, come home with us. I know Shad wants to see the work on the conservatory that I'm not supposed to know about. Don't worry about Harry.'

'Worry about him! I'm not worried about him! I hate him! I love him to distraction!'

'You're spilling brandy on the bed.' She steadies the glass in my hand. 'If you had told him before none of this would have happened. But do you think you will enjoy running a hotel?'

'I won't ever know,' I blubber. 'Why did he follow me to Wallace's lodgings?'

'I don't think he did. He would have arrived sooner.' Charlotte's sensible words are spoiled by a hiccup. 'But I am full of admiration that even at fifteen you knew it to be a false marriage. You were very brave.'

'I had no choice. I was ruined anyway.' A fresh set of tears rise. 'What could I have done? I loved Wallace, silly girl that I was. It was only when he went abroad that I realized I was abandoned and must fend for myself.'

The door bangs open to reveal Shad struggling out of his coat. 'In my bed again, Sophie? Would I were a bachelor. Out, ma'am. You may sleep with the children in the nursery.' He starts on the buttons of his waistcoat. 'The good news, however, is that Wallace has cried off the duel as we thought he would. Why is there a brandy bottle in the bed?'

'Possibly for the same reason that you reek of the stuff yourself,' Charlotte says. 'Where is Harry?'

'He leaves for London at first light. Sophie, pray go to bed and do not make an attempt to find Harry. I have never known a pair so incompetent at making and accepting a proposal of marriage.'

'I don't want to see him.' I lurch to my feet, grabbing on to a bedpost for support. 'I don't want to marry him.'

A footman, embarrassed by my weeping and drunkenness, escorts me to the nursery. Shad and Charlotte are taking no chances with me now and I am so weary and heartsick I don't care. Let them do with me what they will.

Letters fly back and forth in the next couple of days.

I see letters from Shad to Harry in the hall, awaiting collection, and find out that Harry still acts as his agent, hiring new staff. Shad does not offer, and neither do I suggest, that I write to him.

'Well, Amelia,' Shad says at breakfast one morning, an opened letter in his hand, 'I have heard from the Wiltons on your behalf. They would be delighted if you joined them in Bath, as you originally intended.'

'Oh, yes,' Amelia says. 'Poor Jane Wilton must miss me terribly.'

I doubt whether that little giggler misses anything that is not in her immediate vicinity, but Amelia doesn't sound very enthusiastic at the prospect of leaving Brighton. Why should she? Brighton is far more fashionable, and sea bathing infinitely preferable to the cloudy, steamy waters of the old-fashioned city of Bath.

'Perhaps you should go,' Shad says. 'Sophie could travel with you, if she's willing.' He cocks an eyebrow at me. It's early in the morning, and his immediate family are the only ones awake, our hosts keeping more fashionable hours. His sons squirm on his lap, allowed the privilege of breakfasting away from the nursery, and dip pieces of toast into their father's tea.

'As you wish, sir,' I reply and pour him tea into a fresh cup, his present one being almost entirely soggy crumbs.

'Yes, brother,' Amelia says, eyes downcast. 'I fear I have a cold and am not well enough to travel yet.'

But later she mutters to me, 'Sophie, I must return to London. I shall not run away, I swear it, but I must go. Can you help me?'

The only way I can help her at the moment, until her brother agrees to my idea to become a patron of a reputable theatre, is to continue to instruct her in music and teach her some of the skills she will need: how to make herself appear taller on the stage, or older, or younger; how to make the quietest whisper resonate around the house.

And I absolutely refuse to tell her of my life as a courtesan – she does not ask outright but I know she is curious – stressing that I was not a good enough actress; I was not dedicated enough nor did I work hard enough to establish myself successfully in a career on the stage. I do not tell her that I had but half of her talent for fear she will overreach herself.

Charlotte and Shad are most kind to me, treating me as though I were an invalid or an elderly aunt who needs cosseting. They provide special treats, ices, and visits to the circulating library; they encourage me to bathe to lift my spirits. The water is cold and I do not see what good it can possibly do me as I flounder in a garment like a sack and have my face slapped by waves. Charlotte insists I look the better for it. She most certainly does and she and Shad cast each other languishing glances and brush hands when we are in company.

Our hosts, the Earl and Countess of Beresford, enjoy entertaining on a grand scale, and I find myself slipping down to the servants' quarters on those nights. There I discover that Mr Hoskins the butler has a fine singing voice, the third maidservant believes herself to be with child (she is not: I ask some pertinent questions), and the boy who brings in the vegetables longs to read and write.

I arrange for Mr Hoskins to teach him, and whet his appetite by reading *Robinson Crusoe* aloud to him. I wonder if Harry was like this as a boy, bright and ambitious and greedy for knowledge.

I dare not think of my future. Maybe I should visit the gentleman in the City who handles my investments and consider retirement, setting myself up in a very modest sort of way in a small house, but I doubt I can afford to live in London and I cannot see myself anywhere else.

The former fashionable and dashing Mrs Wallace cries quite a lot and sleeps in the nursery. She wakes very early each morning to find small children tweaking her hair and pushing her eyelids open with gentle but insistent fingers.

She is not happy, but she is not unhappy either.

But I know this cannot last, and so one day I ask both Shad and Beresford for advice.

Harry

'There's a legal gentleman to see you, sir.'

I look up from the ledgers over which I have laboured this past week, well pleased that despite my late father's haphazard ciphering and dreadful writing, the hotel runs, mostly, at a profit. Arithmetic does not mend a broken heart but it almost makes me believe in an orderly universe where things are what they seem and an added column of figures gives the same result whether you start from the top or the bottom.

Jack, the waiter who has delivered the news, lounges at the doorway to the office, one ankle crossed over the other, but jumps smartly to attention as I focus on him. I am glad to see the cloth hung over his arm is clean and so are his hands.

A legal gentleman. This does not bode well. Have we poisoned a guest recently? Smothered someone in one of our beds?

'On behalf of Lord Shadderly,' Jack offers.

Even worse. Has something gone horribly wrong with the renovations I supervised for twenty minutes? Did the butler and nursemaid I hired for Lord Shad run amok?

But a plump, snuff-sprinkled form pushes his way into my office, beaming, hand held out. 'Your servant, sir! Geoffrey Trelaise.'

He is a younger son of one of the many branches of the family, it appears, a very distant branch, for this gentleman bears no resemblance to the handsome, lean members of the Trelaise family that I have met. We go through the formalities, I offer refreshment, and push my ledgers aside.

'Well now!' Trelaise says. 'I've heard many good things about you, sir, many good things. Lord and Lady

Shad send their kindest regards. I am here to clear the name of a lady, sir.'

I'm not sure whether I feel relief or foreboding. 'And would that lady be Sophie Wallace?'

'Miss Sophie Marsden, yes, sir.'

I debate whether I should throw this undoubted imposter out and he sees my hesitation – this jocund member of the legal profession may behave like a genial fool, but I think I should not underestimate him.

He continues, 'But what am I thinking? Here, sir, are my credentials, a letter of introduction from the Earl of Beresford.'

The letter bears Beresford's seal and indeed introduces the family lawyer to me.

I lay the letter on my desk and say, 'Why do you refer to the lady by her maiden name?'

'Read these, sir. They are copies, but as you see, witnessed and all made good, from the legal gentleman who represents that personage.' He lays a finger to one nostril and winks.

Another flourish, like a conjuror producing a flock of doves, and another document appears on my desk. And another.

Trelaise rises. 'I shall leave you to peruse these documents, sir. I have a fancy to visit your taproom, for I have heard the punch at Bishop's Hotel is the best in London.'

I show him to the taproom and order punch – my mother sails forth to concoct it, for she feels she best honours my father's memory by attempting to duplicate his fiendish brew – and return to read the documents.

I don't know what to believe. There is an account, from a Mr Buckle, of a false marriage at which he impersonated a vicar, some ten years ago, between Sophie Marsden and Rupert Wallace.

So the marriage is false. She is not married to him and she tried to tell me.

I may have been a fool at fifteen to elope with that man, but I assure you I have not been one since, not for any man.

But then – statements of investments, of earnings from a small house in an unfashionable part of London, leased to a physician and his family – all in the name of Sophie Marsden, *femme seule*. Not a huge amount of wealth, but enough that an adventurer like Captain Wallace might want to lay his hands on it. The lady withdraws nothing, prudently reinvesting. I see her strategy is to build a comfortable income for the future.

And it is this that persuades me, more than any protestation of love or vow of fidelity. She has entrusted me with her deepest secret – not her lovers or her indiscretions, but her financial holdings, the symbol of her independence.

The last item is something wrapped in a scrap of

paper and sealed, again with Beresford's seal. I break the wax and discover a small, pale green object. A piece of glass, battered by its journey through sand and sea-water and transformed into an object of beauty, that Sophie picked up from the beach at Brighton.

I bundle the documents together and return to the taproom where Trelaise and my mother, both of them pink-cheeked and giggling, are working their way through a large amount of punch.

'More ginger, do you think, sir?' My mother raises a glass to me. 'Mr Trelaise says he has brought you good news, but he is very discreet.' That means she'll force the news from me later.

'Dear lady, Mr Bishop, your health. And may I anticipate a happy union in Mr Bishop's future?' Trelaise raises a glass.

'It's about time!' My mother pours me a glass of punch. We drink a toast to . . . I'm not sure who, for the next few hours pass in a happy blur.

Sophie

I return from Bath somewhat travel-weary and still concerned for Amelia, who clearly obeys her brother out of duty and making sure everyone knows she takes very little pleasure in it. Even the fulsome greeting of giggling

Miss Jane Wilton failed to produce much liveliness in her, although she cheered up a little at the prospect of shopping.

Having submitted myself to Mrs Wilton's contempt for ten minutes in her drawing room (I think the lady debated whether she should send me downstairs to the kitchen), I retired to the very respectable hotel the Trelaise family patronize when visiting that town, and subjected myself to some bowing and scraping. Yet I cannot help but notice the waiter who wipes his nose on his sleeve and the greasy fingerprints on the wine glass (I send it back) and think of Bishop's Hotel. I wonder how Mrs Bishop fares and whether Harry has started his campaign to smarten the place up.

And then I take the coach back to Norfolk, a long journey which gives me much time for reflection, and I am glad indeed when I arrive at the crossroads. The wind ripples through the marshy grasses and skylarks twitter overhead; the occasional tree etched against the sky takes on a particular beauty in its isolation.

Ahead of me I see a familiar group of figures, Charlotte and her two sons, waving wildly at me, followed by a female servant who must be the new nursemaid carrying the infant Harriet.

'My dear Sophie!' She embraces me and the two little boys crowd around me, asking if I have brought them presents. 'I trust you are not too fatigued from your journey? I could send Martha back for the trap, if you like.'

'No need. I am cramped from sitting in that coach for so long. How is the conservatory?'

'Splendid. John threw a cricket ball through one of the window panes and I thought Shad would kill him.' She takes my arm. 'Was Amelia still in a sulk? I really don't know what to do with her although Shad talks of sending her to his fashionable sister in London for the season.'

I take Harriet so the nursemaid can take my bag and carry her upon my hip as we walk to the house. We dissuade the little boys from dabbling in the duckpond and John, who has taken over the duties of looking after Amelia's poultry, waves to us, a basket of eggs in his other hand.

As we enter the cobbled yard surrounded by outbuildings at the side of the house (for we do not stand on formality, choosing to use the side door rather than the front door), we are greeted by Mark the footman, who wears his largest hook and seems to be directing Luke and Matthew in the transportation of some unwieldy piece of timber.

When he sees us, a furtive expression comes over his face, and he grabs the door of the nearest building and pushes Luke and Matthew and their burden inside. Thumps and cries of pain as they encounter obstacles emerge from behind the closed door, along with the shouts of an enraged woman.

'What on earth are they doing?'

She shrugs. 'Oh, Shad asked them to take some old things out of the attic, I believe.'

'Into the dairy?' I glance at Mark who stands against the door, arms spread against the wood as though at any moment we will break the door down and he must protect the contents at all cost. Inside, someone shrieks that these great oafs will spoil her butter.

'It is strange,' Charlotte murmurs.

'You're plotting something. And why is there a fire lit in the steward's house?' For a trickle of smoke emerges from the chimney. 'Is Harry here?'

'Oh, no! Certainly not! He is in London. Yes, at his hotel,' she says with tremendous emphasis, and I am relieved indeed that she does not need to make her living on the stage.

I hand Harriet back to her mother and march to the door of the house. I rap smartly on the wood but receive no answer. So I push open the door.

I've never been in Harry's house before, and I look around with great curiosity. Some cleaning seems to be taking place, for all the furniture is huddled up at one end of the single room that is a combined kitchen and parlour, and the bedchamber, the other room of the house, is completely bare.

But Harry's possessions are still here: a steadily ticking clock on the mantelpiece, and a few books, a pen, and a bottle of ink on the small table pushed against the wall. Bundles of herbs hang from the ceiling and at the hearth a kettle, hissing and releasing a little steam, stands on a trivet. His spare coat, the one that is a little too large for him – a gift from Shad – hangs on a hook on the bedchamber door. I press my face against the wool and then against the silk lining, wishing it was still warm from his body.

The room is stark, with plain whitewashed walls, floors swept and scrubbed to a creamy smoothness. The small window, with ancient thick glass in diamond-shaped panes, looks out on to green fields.

And on the windowsill, as though echoing that wavering and uncertain green, lies a piece of glass, smoothed, transformed, made magic by unknown storms.

I leave the house and walk towards the dairy, where the milkmaid continues to harangue her unwelcome guests and Mark still stands guard.

'Get your foot out of that, 'tis ruined!'

'Don't you worry, Molly,' tain't a real leg.'

'Girt great oaf, you think that makes it better? Cook'll have the skin off your back.'

More thumps and the sound of a breaking vessel.

Mark presses himself against the door, his hook actually buried in the wood of the lintel.

'I know what you're doing,' I say. 'And I know you won't tell me where Mr Bishop is, though I daresay he's close by, but you don't have to hide from me. Pray continue.'

He answers with a smile that probably almost matches the one on my face, nods, and wrenches his hook out with a great splintering sound. 'Come on out, then, lads. We're discovered.'

Harry

It's time.

I have admired the new conservatory, made my farewells to the staff, and given instructions to the new steward. I advise him that any seamen seeking employment must be hired immediately even if they are bereft of skills or limbs, shake his hand, and wish him luck.

I accept Shad's invitation to dine with the family later that evening and return to the steward's house. My replacement will probably not occupy the house for a few days, for I have some unfinished business before my departure for London.

Molly, our milkmaid, passes me, a large bowl of cream balanced on her hip. She pauses to curtsy, her deference spoiled by a saucy wink.

She knows.

Outside the dairy the cats have gathered to lick up a patch of mingled butter and cream that bears footmarks and the imprint of a wooden leg.

And so to the house, where the tick of the clock sounds louder than usual, the rays of the late afternoon sun slanting in through the mullioned windows.

The bedchamber door is closed.

I open it to find the room occupied entirely by one monstrous piece of furniture I know well. The bed is huge and ancient, its posts dark with age and carved with leaves and flowers, the hangings a dark red silk. A bed made for passion.

The occupant of the bed, who mirrors in her state of undress the cavorting deities of the tester, smiles and holds out her hand to me.

'Sir,' Sophie says. 'I must speak to you about my bed.'

Pick up a *little black dress* – it's a girl thing.

THE TRUE NAOMI STORY
A.M. Goldsher
PB £5.99

Naomi Braver is catapulted from waiting tables to being the new rock sensation overnight. But stardom isn't all it's cracked up to be . . . Can Naomi master the game of fame before it's too late?

A rock'n'roll romance about one girl's journey to stardom

978 0 7553 3992 1

FORGET ABOUT IT
Caprice Crane
PB £5.99

When Jordan Landeua is hit by a car, she seizes the opportunity to start over and fakes amnesia. But just as she's said goodbye to Jordan the pushover, the unthinkable happens and she has to start over for real. Will she remember in time what truly makes her happy?

978 0 7553 4204 4

Pick up a *little black dress* – it's a girl thing.

THE FARMER NEEDS A WIFE
Janet Gover
PBO £5.99

Rural romances become all the rage when editor Helen Woodley starts a new magazine column profiling Australia's lovelorn farmers. But a lot of people (and Helen herself) are about to find out that the course of true love ain't ever smooth . . .

978 0 7553 4715 5

It's not all haystacks and pitchforks, ladies – get ready for a scorching outback read!

HIDE YOUR EYES
Alison Gaylin
PBO £5.99

Samantha Leiffer's in big trouble: the chest she saw a sinister man dumping into the Hudson river contained a dead body, meaning she's now a witness in a murder case. It's just as well hot, hard-line detective John Krull is by her side . . .

978 0 7553 4802 2

'Alison Gaylin is my new must-read' Harlen Coben

Pick up a *little black dress* – it's a girl thing.

IMPROPER RELATIONS
Janet Mullany
£5.99

After losing her best friend and cousin Ann Weller in marriage to the Earl of Beresford, sharp-witted Charlotte Hayden is even ruder than usual to potential suitors. Introduced to Beresford's wayward cousin, Shad, Charlotte may have met her match in witty repartee – but he's hardly husband material and a hasty marriage of convenience might have been a mistake . . .

978 0 7553 4780 3

Another fabulous regency romp through crossed wires and illicit liaisons!

978 0 7553 3280 9

BLUE CHRISTMAS
Mary Kay Andrews
£5.99

Eloise Foley is looking forward to a magical Christmas filled with friends, family and festive fun, but it doesn't seem as if everyone around her is feeling the same seasonal goodwill.

Will Eloise get the fairy-tale celebration she desires or is she heading for a blue Christmas?

Pick up a *little black dress* – it's a girl thing.

ABOUT TIME
Niamh Shaw
£5.99

Why is Lara so nervous about moving to New York with boy-friend Barry? Of course, there *is* the small matter of forgetting about socially inept super-geek Conn, who has an annoying habit of making repeat appearances in her love life. It's about time she put the past behind her. Although that's easier said than done . . .

978 0 7553 4857 2

HEN NIGHT PROPHECIES: HARD TO GET
Jessica Fox
£5.99

Charlotte loves her job at the Arts Council – it's just a shame she has to share the office with her ex-husband, who also happens to be dating her boss. Fate, hope and charity influence Charlotte's romantic destiny as the third prophecy in the addictive HEN NIGHT PROPHECIES series is revealed: *'Love will come through hope alone.'*

978 0 7553 4959 3

Pick up a *little black dress* – it's a girl thing.

SARIS IN THE CITY
Rekha Waheed
£5.99

When ambitious City analyst Yasmin Yusuf's hope for a traditional 'happy ever after' in the romance stakes is shattered she decides there's only one course of action: get smart, sexy and successful, and what better way to do this than by saving a failing lingerie business?

978 0 7553 5613 3

A fabulous feisty novel – East meets West in Rekha Waheed's brilliant romance.

UNLUCKY IN LOVE
Jessica Fox
£6.99

Risk-taker Libby Foster wishes she thought things through more – maybe then she'd avoid being humiliated at work over her reckless romantic attachments. So it's just as well that she's swearing herself off men and escaping to a Thai island, where nothing could possibly go wrong . . .

The fourth novel in this addictive new series, THE HEN NIGHT PROPHECIES, focuses on Libby, '*A danger to men . . .*'

978 0 7553 4960 9

You can buy any of these other
Little Black Dress titles from your
bookshop or *direct from the publisher*.

FREE P&P AND UK DELIVERY
(Overseas and Ireland £3.50 per book)

TO ORDER SIMPLY CALL THIS NUMBER

01235 400 414

or visit our website: www.headline.co.uk

Prices and availability subject to change without notice.